Veterinarian's Date with a Billionaire

ANJ

Press

Pittsburgh

Veterinarian's Date with a Billionaire
ANJ Press, First edition. June 2019.
Copyright © 2019 Amelia Addler.
Written by Amelia Addler.

Cover design by Charmaine Ross at CharmaineRoss.com

For Andrzej
my brave, funny, silly, and loving dog
who is fighting cancer with all of his might.

I would go to the moon and back to save you.

Chapter 1

It didn't take long for Juliet to spot her friends laughing in a booth at the far corner of the restaurant. They didn't see her coming. A smile spread across her face as she walked toward them.

"Well, well, well," she said, arms crossed. "If it isn't the Dynamic Duo of Wayside High School."

"No," Greg replied, standing from his seat. "With you, we're the Three Stooges."

Juliet broke into laughter. "I completely forgot that they used to call us that." She pulled Greg in for a hug.

Aaron stood up, wrapping his arms around them both in a group hug.

"When did you get so strong?" squeaked Juliet.

Aaron shrugged. "I have to be able to hold a wriggling four-year-old twin in each arm, and I think that's the ultimate workout."

"Oh my gosh, I haven't gotten to see them since their third birthday party. I haven't seen you guys in forever!" said Juliet as she took a seat.

Greg shook his head. "No, that's not true. We all hung out six months ago, at my wedding. And my bachelor party, though the kids weren't there."

"Ah, of course. How could I forget?"

How *could* she forget? She was the only woman invited on the bachelor party – a four day backpacking trip in the mountains. She was worried that she wouldn't be able to keep up, but she was one of the fastest in the pack. It seemed that getting married and having kids really slowed the rest of her friends down.

"So Jules," said Greg, "What's this project that you need help with?"

She took a deep breath. "It's a long story, but basically, the vet clinic where I work is at risk of being shut down."

They looked at her with surprise, and she was about to continue when something caught her eye. It looked like...but no, it couldn't be.

Greg turned around to see what she was squinting at. "What?"

"Shh!" She kicked him under the table. "Turn around!"

Greg snapped back to face her just as Aaron leaned across the table to see what was so interesting.

"Could you guys be any more obvious? I thought I saw someone, but – it turns out I was wrong."

Aaron shrugged. "It's the Wednesday before Thanksgiving. We probably know everybody in this restaurant. It's practically a high school reunion."

Juliet cautioned a glance toward the front door again. She was being silly; there was no one there and she'd gotten all flustered for nothing.

She cleared her throat and started again. "We had grant funding from – "

A voice cut her off from behind. "Hey guys! How's it going?"

Her eyes didn't deceive her. She'd know that voice anywhere: her ex-boyfriend, James Balin.

"Hey man! Long time no see. How's it going?" Greg offered a handshake before motioning for James to take a seat.

That flushed feeling was back, and Juliet knew that the skin on her chest was bright red under her hoodie. This was the *last* thing she thought she'd have to face during this visit to her hometown.

Her mom nagging her about her hair being too long? Yes, always. The owner of the restaurant scolding her, for the thousandth time, about breaking a huge stack of dishes back when she was a freshman in high school? Sure.

But running into James? Definitely not. As far as she knew, he hadn't been back to Michigan in years. His family didn't even live there anymore. It made her feel a little rattled to see him appear like that. But she didn't want him thinking that he could rattle her, so she needed to play it cool.

Juliet turned to him and smiled with as much grace as she could muster. He hadn't aged a day – well, not in a normal way, more like a George Clooney way. His blue eyes were as bright as ever, and she had to force herself not to stare. James had many flaws, but being homely was not one of them.

"Pretty good, it's good to see you all," James said. His eyes met Juliet's. "Do you mind if I join you?"

Before she could think of an excuse as to why he couldn't sit with them, Aaron said, "No, of course not!"

She reminded herself to breathe slowly. This was the problem with having guy friends. It was all fine and dandy until an ex-boyfriend showed up. If Juliet's female friends were there, they would've known that the ex-boyfriend protocol called for civility with a large helping of coldness.

They wouldn't shake his hand. They wouldn't ask how he was doing – unless they planned to look away, disinterested in his answer. And they certainly wouldn't have invited him to sit down!

James scooted into the booth next to Greg.

"Hi James, fancy seeing you here," she said coolly.

"Yeah, I'm in town, kinda a surprise actually. Zach invites me for Thanksgiving every year, and I finally took him up on it."

Juliet shifted uncomfortably to make sure her legs didn't brush against his; there wasn't enough room in the booth for another person.

"Oh yeah? How's he doing?" asked Aaron.

"Really well," replied James. "I haven't been able to see him for a while, so it's a nice treat."

Juliet had to force herself not to say something snarky back to him, like "I'm sure it is hard to see your best friend when you refuse to leave your precious New York City."

Instead, she said, "Is your dad alone for Thanksgiving?"

James laughed. "No, he's got all of his coworkers to keep him company. They're working on a big presentation for some investors, I doubt they'll take any breaks for Thanksgiving dinner. Or Christmas."

"I see."

"It's so nice to see you Juliet, I can't believe I ran into you here," said James.

What was he going on about? Where else would she be for Thanksgiving? Oh – yeah, she could be with her boyfriend's family. If she had a boyfriend.

"Yeah, it's nice to see you too," she lied.

Greg prompted her again. "So what's going on with the clinic?"

"Oh!" James said, eyes lighting up. "Are you working at a clinic here?"

"Westside Veterinary Clinic," she said, keeping the edge out of her tone. "In Lansing."

It was best to remain neutral, she decided. She'd carry on as though he wasn't even there, or as though it wasn't the first time she'd seen him in five years. It'd been so long that it was just like seeing a stranger. At least that's what she told herself to keep from getting frazzled.

"We got notice two months ago that our funding will run out at the end of the year, and it won't be renewed. The grant agency is no longer able to fund vet clinics."

Aaron shook his head. "That's awful. How long can the clinic survive without funding?"

Juliet sighed. "A month? Maybe two? Not very long. We don't make much profit, because everything we do is offered on a sliding scale based on people's income. It's not enough to cover operating costs – hence why we got the grant for being a vet clinic in an under-served area."

"That's so nice though," interjected James. "You're helping, uh, poor people take care of their pets?"

She turned to him with the slightest glare in her eye. "When you say it like that you make them sound like they're homeless. They just don't have a lot of extra money to spend on their pets. But it doesn't mean that they love them any less."

"Of course not," James added, shaking his head.

Juliet turned back to her friends. "But I came up with a plan. There is this newish company that develops cancer drugs. They're not huge, but one of their drugs has been out for years. At first, it was only available for use in animals, but now it's undergoing human trials. They're holding a contest to raise awareness for how well the drug works. The winner of the contest will get one million dollars for a veterinary clinic, plus a stipend to run clinical trials."

Aaron raised his eyebrows. "That's incredible. What's in it for them?"

"Well, they want people to put together a video of animals that were saved by the drug. They're going to use that for marketing and fundraising, I don't know."

James nodded. "It's actually really smart. This can create a lot of hype, even beyond the winning video. It'll help them with investment and buy in, more than a million dollars in advertising could do alone."

Before Juliet had the chance to cut him off, Aaron asked, "Does your dad's company have something like that?"

James shook his head. "No, we have an in-house marketing department who spends *plenty* of money on their own. Plus, none of the drugs that we developed are used in animals, just in people. But it's not a bad idea."

"Anyways," Juliet said, "I contacted a lot of my old vet school friends who are at some of the bigger veterinary practices. They've been using this drug for years and some of their patients agreed to appear in a video about it. Which is where I come in. I'm going to make this video and win the contest. I hope."

Greg smiled and patted the dark bag sitting on the table. "I brought my old camera, just like you asked. It's all yours."

Aaron leaned back, crossing his arms. "And Greg is going to edit this video for you, right?"

Juliet shrugged, a smile on her lips. "No, I can't afford to pay him."

Greg laughed. "Oh, please. It would be nice to edit something other than wedding videos for once. And it's an honor to loan my skills to your vet clinic for poor people."

Juliet had to swallow to suppress the laugh that almost sprung from her chest. Maybe guy friends had *some* merits.

"Thanks Greg, that means a lot," said Juliet.

"I know a good bit about how drug companies work," James said, apparently missing Greg's jab at him. "Maybe I could be of some help?"

"I think I'll be okay," replied Juliet.

She was unable to force herself to smile this time. Why did James think he could show up in town after all these years and act like he was just another member of the gang? Did he think that she'd look at him and want to be friends all of a sudden?

Luckily, at that moment, Zach came over to their table. "Hey guys, good to see you."

Everyone smiled and said their hello's. Juliet made a point of being much warmer to Zach than she was to James. She liked Zach, after all. It wasn't his fault that his best friend was a jerk.

"James – we're going to put our dinner orders in soon. Do you want to come over or...?"

"Oh, of course. Sorry, sure." James stood from the table. "It was really nice catching up with you guys. Maybe I'll see you later?"

"Sure, see you later," said Aaron.

Juliet waited until they were out of earshot to speak again. "Thanks a lot guys," she hissed. "I really wanted to have to pretend to be nice to my ex-boyfriend."

Greg and Aaron started laughing.

"What's so funny?" she said, deciding again that guy friends were no good.

"I don't think that anyone would think that you were trying to be nice to him."

She crossed her arms. "What's that supposed to mean? And why did you tell him to sit down?"

Greg shrugged. "I didn't want to be rude. And besides, it's been a long time. Maybe it's time for you to forgive? You can forgive but not forget."

"You know I hate that phrase."

"Yeah, we know," Aaron said with a grin. "Maybe it's time to get over it?"

"No! It's a stupid phrase! If you forgive, but you still hang onto whatever they did, then that's not really forgiveness, is it?"

Greg shrugged. "I mean, it's a form of forgiveness."

"No, it's not forgiveness," Juliet said matter-of-factly.

"Okay then, just forgive and forget," said Aaron.

Juliet realized that her shoulders were scrunched halfway up to her ears. She released the tension. "There are some things that can't be forgiven."

Aaron and Greg looked at each other, then back at Juliet.

"You're still *that* mad?" asked Aaron. "I don't think that's good for your health."

Greg tried to hide his smile behind a menu.

She wasn't going to play into their teasing anymore. "I'm not mad. I just keep a very updated list of people to be avoided."

"Like a black book with people you hate?" asked Greg.

Juliet sighed. "No, I don't 'hate' anybody. There are just certain people that you can never trust."

Aaron got a very serious look on his face. "We better be careful, or we'll end up on her list."

Greg nodded. "It's kinda like a Do Not Call list. But it's worse – a Do Not Trust list."

Juliet threw a sugar packet at him. "You're both going to end up on my Do Not Call list soon."

They laughed and finally moved onto another topic.

The rest of the evening was nice, even though Juliet felt like her nerves were on edge. She constantly looked to see if James was going to sneak up on them again. Luckily, he didn't, and after they paid their tab, they walked out to the parking lot together without any sign of James.

Aaron made them all promise to stop by his house after Thanksgiving dinner, and they agreed. Juliet waved goodbye, still on alert that James could show up at any minute. She quickly started her car and was about to pull away from her parking spot when the car suddenly stopped.

"What in the world?"

She tried turning the key in the ignition again, but that didn't do anything. She put her foot on the gas with no response. She realized that everything in the car was dark – even the clock stopped glowing. She pulled the emergency brake and got out to take a look at it.

Greg and Aaron were still chatting and came over to see what was going on.

"What happened?" asked Greg.

"I have no idea. It was going, and then all of a sudden, it wasn't."

"Maybe I could take a look?" said a new voice.

Juliet closed her eyes. Of course James found her again. Just when she was about to get away from him for good.

Chapter 2

James took a step forward and opened the hood of Juliet's Saturn Vue. He didn't know much about cars, so he wasn't really sure what he was looking at, but he still wanted to try. He would do anything for a chance to talk to Juliet for just a bit longer.

Luckily for him, Aaron took the lead with the car. "Well, your oil looks okay. I don't see anything obviously wrong, but Juliet, this is a pretty old car. It might be the engine or the transmission."

She put her hands on her hips. "It can't be broken right now. Why couldn't it break *next* week? I have to drive to Ann Arbor on Friday – it was the only day the lady with the parrot could meet."

James saw his chance. "I have the whole week off. I could drive you anywhere you need to go."

She responded without looking at him. "Thanks, but I'm sure my car just needs some type of fluid or something and it'll be back up and running."

"I'm not sure about that Jules," Greg said, shifting his weight. "And you're gonna have a hard time finding a car to rent the day after Thanksgiving."

James tried to suppress a smile. Clearly Greg didn't hold a grudge as long as Juliet did.

"It wouldn't be the worst thing for you to have someone go with you," Aaron added. "You don't know the people you're going to meet. What if one of them attacks you or something?"

"Why would anyone attack me? I'm sure they're all nice, normal people. Since when are you so paranoid?"

Greg shrugged. "Better safe than sorry, don't you think?"

A vein bulged from Juliet's forehead, but she didn't respond. She got back into the driver's seat and turned her key in the ignition again. The car didn't even try to start.

James felt almost giddy with excitement.

"I can give you a ride back to your parents' house if you like," he said.

"No thank you," she responded. "Greg – their house is on your way home. You don't mind, do you?"

"No, of course not. Let's go."

"My offer to drive you on Friday stands!" James yelled after her. "You still have my number, right?"

"No, I deleted it," she shouted without looking back.

He frowned. This wasn't going to be easy, but he knew that when he made the decision to come back to Michigan. "I'll text you so you can let me know if you need my help."

She got into the passenger seat of Greg's car without responding. James watched as they pulled away.

Although it wasn't exactly a warm welcome, it was still a better interaction than he expected. Juliet was a tough cookie – it was one of the things he loved most about her.

Yet it wasn't easy for him to face her. He couldn't go a day without thinking of her, but he was afraid of her, too. So instead of doing the brave thing and telling her how he felt, he found ways to distract himself.

His job was one of the few things that could keep his mind occupied. It worked – for a while, at least. He never allowed himself to take a break. He knew that taking a break would mean he'd have time to think, and if he had time to think, loneliness and regret would engulf him. One year, he spent so much time traveling and meeting investors that he spent a total of three weeks at home.

He could feel himself growing thin, but he *couldn't* stop. Instead, he started slipping at work. His presentations got sloppy. He forgot to send in orders. His father was perpetually disappointed with him, at one point dubbing him a "brainless wonder" who needed to be "studied for the good of humanity."

That was a *bit* harsh. It all started eating away at James, and everything came to a head the week before Thanksgiving. He was supposed to meet with one of their oldest investors to give them an update on the company's metrics. It wasn't a huge challenge, but the pressure was intense. Losing the investor could endanger the company – a fact that his dad made sure to tell him when he reminded him to "pack a brain" for the trip.

So naturally, James stayed up too late the night before the meeting. He was anxious, burnt out and brittle. He couldn't fall asleep and ended up watching *The Great British Baking Show* for five straight episodes. The premise was delightful; there was no competitive nastiness between the contestants and the bakers were so passionate. It was the opposite of his job.

The next day, he overslept and completely missed the meeting. When he showed up three hours late, he tried to sneak into the building, only to be escorted out by security.

Word got back to his dad rather quickly about what happened. James got to hear that he was a disappointment, a failure, and that he endangered the company and the jobs of everyone there. To James, it very much sounded like he was fired, which was problematic, because he was supposed to take over the company when his dad retired.

Yet somehow, when he thought me might be fired, he didn't feel upset. His heart soared. Being fired meant freedom. He no longer had to work at a job that he didn't care about and towards goals that meant nothing to him.

He knew that he couldn't work any harder, no matter how many rude nicknames his dad made up for him. The job made him unhappy – no, his own choices made him unhappy. The job was just one of them. James realized that he had to face the poor choices he'd made and try to undo them.

So instead of arguing with his dad, he decided to run away without another word between them.

Well – that wasn't exactly true. It wasn't *exactly* running away. He felt guilty for not seeing his best friend for over three years, so that was part of his decision to flee New York. Also, he could better wait out his father's temper tantrum by removing himself from the city.

But the real reason was more than that. Much more than that – it had to do with someone that popped into his mind whenever he went for a long run or woke up before his alarm. It was something that nagged him late at night and when he sat down to eat dinner alone.

Maybe his dad was right, and he was a failure and a "brainless wonder." James didn't know, and he didn't much care anymore. His own spectacular failure freed him from the need to be successful at work.

What he did know was that after five years, he still wasn't over Juliet. He knew that he would never be over her. It was the only thing he was sure of – Juliet McCarron was the love of his life. He took a wrong turn when he lost her and he would do anything to win her back.

And so far, it was going much better than he could have ever planned. Juliet was at the Two Rivers Grille, just like Zach said she would be. Of course, she looked *amazing*. She wasn't trying to, naturally – she was in a hooded sweatshirt, her long blonde hair pulled back into a loose ponytail – and it only added to her charm.

Sure, she wasn't thrilled to see him, but he expected that. James knew that she wouldn't welcome him with open arms. He hoped that maybe she'd missed him too, but her feigned indifference was okay. It wasn't Juliet's way to forgive easily. He fully intended to apologize for how he'd hurt her in the past, knowing that the hardest part would be getting her to talk to him in the first place.

It was unbelievably lucky that her car broke down. It was so brilliant that he worried that she may even accuse him of doing something to her car. He never would've done that – but he was thrilled that the universe offered him a helping hand in the matter anyway.

He pulled out his phone and found her in his list of contacts. How many times did he pull her name up, press CALL and then hang up? How many times did he have a message typed out, only to delete it?

Hopefully she hadn't changed her phone number since they last spoke – if so, he still knew the number for her parents' house.

He typed out a text message: "Hi Juliet, this is James with your free taxi service. We're running a special this week for the low cost of zero dollars. Please respond to this message if you are interested."

He hit send and smiled. That would crack her up, right?

Three hours later and no answer. He decided to send one more message. "Please also respond if you are not interested, as we have many parties creating inspiring veterinary videos in need of the service."

He stayed up late that night, hoping that she might write back. She did not.

James got up early the next morning and helped Zach's mom prepare for Thanksgiving dinner. Despite not coming to visit in years, she still treated him like he was family. He didn't have a single friend like that in New York, and he hated himself for not visiting for so long.

There were 24 people coming for dinner that evening, and that meant there was plenty of help needed. James was initially on potato peeling duty, but he was so slow that he was switched to setting up the tables and chairs. It was nice to catch up with Zach and to spend some quality time with Zach's wife Amy – even though Amy's favorite activity was teasing him mercilessly.

Dinner came and went without any response from Juliet. James decided to bring it up to Zach and Amy as they washed and dried dishes.

"Would it be weird if I showed up at her parents' house, just to say hello?"

Zach handed him a bowl to dry. "It would be weird, because you haven't been there in years, and you're not just stopping by to say hello."

James frowned. "True."

The last time that he spoke to Juliet was the night that she broke up with him and refused to speak to him again. He was surprised by the finality of her decision; things were great until that point.

Well, almost – their relationship was wonderful for the first two years when they were both in college. It did get a bit rocky when James graduated and moved to New York City; Juliet still had one year left at school, but he thought that they were strong enough to survive the distance.

James' excitement to start working at his dad's company clouded his judgement; he finally had a chance to prove himself and he didn't think that being apart would be *that* bad. Yet after he started working, their easy relationship became difficult; – there were arguments, tense silences, and a lack of understanding between them.

"What's inspiring you to show up at Juliet's house all of a sudden?" asked Amy.

"It's not quite all of a sudden," James replied. "I haven't stopped thinking about her since we broke up. She's the one that got away."

No matter who he met, no one measured up to her. Dating was tough, though he tried to give it a fair shot. Instead of focusing on whatever his date was telling him, he found himself wondering what Juliet was doing or what she would say about a new movie or TV show.

Though he tried not to, he compared every woman that he met to her. It didn't help that he kept attracting the wrong type of person – women who thought he was into the money, the job title, and the New York partying scene. He wasn't.

If there was a girl like Juliet in New York City, he couldn't find her. There was no one with her never-ending passion, no one with her sharp tongue and tender heart (that was covered with a thin, but hard, shell).

"Aw, that's kind of sweet. How long has it been?" asked Amy.

"A long time," said James. "Five years."

Zach let out a long whistle. "Wow, I did *not* realize that it was that long since you proposed to her."

"You proposed to her!" gasped Amy. "So you were engaged? I never knew that."

"No," James said, tugging at his collar. Was it getting hot in there from all the dish washing? "She turned me down. I made some selfish choices that pushed her away – especially in that last year we were together. There was one in particular that I'm still embarrassed about."

"Do tell," said Amy.

James shook his head. "Not today. I've already revealed enough embarrassing stuff. But I got pretty desperate, I could feel her slipping away, and I was too dumb to put two and two together. I thought all I needed to do was propose to show her how much I loved her."

"Yeah," interjected Zach. "Proposing was *not* the way to communicate your feelings. You should've *actually* communicated your feelings – using words. And not just the words, 'Will you marry me?' "

"So she said no?" Amy leaned back on the sink, taking a break from scrubbing the turkey pan. "And then for five years you didn't even try to talk to her?"

"Of course I tried to talk to her, but she never answered. Not once. So I wanted to respect her decision and try to move on. And then the time flew and...well, yeah, it was stupid. I thought I could get over her. I can't."

Part of the reason why time went so quickly was because James threw himself into his work. If he worked evenings and weekends and holidays, it helped keep his head clear. Also, the more hours he put in, the more that his dad was somewhat happy with him.

Clearly, after a year of Juliet not returning his messages, he should have changed his tactics. But he was afraid – if he actually went to her and asked for a second chance, she could reject him for the final time. If he never asked, the chance was always out there. At least that's what he told himself.

"And now you show up, hoping that Juliet won't be able to resist your cool car," Amy said with a smile.

"No." James laughed. Zach really married quite a firecracker. "In fact, she'd be more likely to agree to travel with me if I had a different car. Juliet is not into flashy stuff."

"Then why did you bring a flashy car here?" asked Zach.

"Well, my dad's kinda angry with me right now for a work related issue. He blocked my access to the garage, and he froze all of my work-related bank accounts and credit cards."

"Whoa," said Amy. "Your dad takes a family feud to the next level."

"He always has. He tells me that it's for my own good, and that if I expect to successfully run a multi-billion dollar company once he's gone, then I need some tough love."

"That's very tough love," said Amy. "I thought my parents were hard on me. All they ever did was send me to my room to think about what I'd done."

"Well," Zach said, "when your son has access to your billions of dollars, you can't really send him to his room. He might, oh, I don't know – fly off to Amsterdam or something. But definitely not to his room."

James rolled his eyes. "That was *one* time. And you loved that trip! You make me sound like a trust fund brat."

"I did love that trip, thanks again bud," Zach conceded. "But don't take this the wrong way. You kind of *are* a trust fund kid. Why don't you have your own bank account?"

"I do have my own bank account!" James protested. "He froze the other one."

Amy snorted. "The *other* one? You know the rest of us don't share bank accounts with our fathers."

"It's a company bank account. For expenses and stuff."

"Uh huh," Zach nodded. "Then how much money do you have in your real bank account? The one where your direct deposits go?"

"There's enough money in there to get by," he said with a frown.

He honestly had no idea. He'd never kept track of money – he didn't need to. James knew that meant he was spoiled, but what was he supposed to do? He wasn't going to turn away company money for company purposes. He barely even slept in his condo in New York because he was always working.

Zach laughed. "I know you don't even know how much money you have in there. I love you man, but that's not normal. And you *did* total your dad's Bentley."

James cringed. "True. But it's just a car. I don't know what he was so mad about."

He was only able to keep a straight face for five seconds before he burst out laughing.

"Okay, yeah, that was pretty bad. But he has like three other ones. And he's always mad at me for something. It doesn't matter what I do."

"Why don't you just talk to him?" said Amy. "It sounds like you guys have a lot of anger and not a lot of communication."

James took a stack of dishes and loaded them back into the cupboard. "It's hard. He's been very closed off since my mom died. He wants me to do well, but I don't know what that means, so he gets angry. And then I act out, and here we are."

"Stop being a big teenager," said Zach. "You guys have been fighting this way since you were 13."

"I know, but I'm not going to be the first one to budge," said James.

Amy snapped him with a towel.

"Ow! You're really good at that!"

"Listen to Zach!" she said. "One of you has to give in."

James felt his phone buzz in his pocket and reached to grab it. "Well it's not going to be me. Especially because my taxi service may have just gotten its first customer."

Chapter 3

Thanksgiving dinner was a small affair at the McCarron household. Juliet's brother Derrick went to Thanksgiving with his wife's family that year, so it was just Juliet and her parents. She enjoyed spending time with her parents, but it seemed as they got older, they annoyed one another more and more. The big problem this time was that the turkey was too dry.

"I asked your father if the turkey was ready," her mother complained. "Why didn't he go and check?"

"I don't know Mom," said Juliet.

"And now it looks all dried out, look at this skin!"

Juliet glanced over. "It looks fine. I'm sure it'll be good."

Juliet went into the dining room to set the table. Her dad turned off the TV to join her.

"How was I supposed to know that she was asking me to go check on the turkey? She said, 'Do you think it's done?' And I didn't know, so that's what I said. How would I know that it was my responsibility to make sure the turkey didn't get dry?"

"I'm sure it'll be fine," said Juliet. "Let's all stop worrying about the turkey, we haven't even had it yet."

She was trying not to lose her temper, but it was hard. There was a lot of yelling in her house growing up, so yelling was a hard habit for her to break as an adult. It wasn't that her parents didn't love each other – they loved each other very much. But life was always stressful in the McCarron house. Her mom worked at the grocery store and her dad had a small business as a mechanic. Despite both of them working as much as they could, money was always tight. And with both parents constantly overworked, tired, and living paycheck to paycheck, tensions ran high.

It wasn't until Juliet was in high school that she realized that everyone didn't live like that. She was assigned to work on a semester-long project once with a girl named Sarah. Sarah's dad was an engineer. They lived in a big house and had nicer, newer cars that *never* broke down on hot days or made loud noises on the highway.

One time, when Sarah was driving Juliet home from school, she rear-ended another car. Juliet flew into a panic; something like this would lead to weeks of yelling in her house.

To her shock, Sarah's parents showed up and were only worried that the girls were okay. Juliet remembered Sarah's mom saying "It's just a car. It's nothing that money can't fix."

Nothing that money can't fix. From that point on, Juliet wondered if money could fix her family. If there was less stress on everybody, would they be able to stop blowing up at each other? Would there be any more slammed doors? Would her parents be able to sleep at night? Maybe they would all be different people – better people.

It was too late now, though. With Juliet and Derrick moved out on their own, her parents didn't have to worry quite as much about money. Yet their old habits persisted, and then they developed this new routine of complaining about each other to whomever was visiting.

They cut into the turkey; it was dry, as expected. Juliet didn't mind – she preferred to drown everything in gravy anyways. Her mom was never a gifted cook, so Juliet tried to keep ketchup or gravy handy.

The turkey probably wouldn't have been much better if her dad checked on it when he was hinted to do so. She decided to keep that to herself.

"See, would you look at that? It's not supposed to be like that," her mom groaned.

"Well next time how about you say 'Hey George, I need you to go check on the turkey.' "

"Because," responded her mother, "I shouldn't have to *tell* you to do everything."

Juliet decided to change the topic. "So Dad, did you figure out what's wrong with my car?"

"I did, but your mother started on me about that turkey as soon as I got out of the shower so I didn't have a chance to tell you."

"Okay, so what's the matter with it?"

He chewed through a big bite of stuffing. "It's done."

"Oh! You fixed it!"

He shook his head. "No, I mean it's broken. For good."

"What! How is that possible? You can fix anything!"

"I can't fix a broken timing belt. You should've let me replace that about 10,000 miles ago."

"Why can't you replace it now?" she said. "I need a car so I can get to Ann Arbor tomorrow for that video that I'm doing for the clinic."

He shoved a large fork full of mashed potatoes into his mouth. "Can't do it. The timing belt broke and damaged the engine. It's game over. Don't you think it's time for a new car anyway? That Saturn is fifteen years old!"

"Yeah, except I won't be able to get a new car in time," Juliet said.

Plus, she was totally broke. Her parents didn't understand why she didn't have a lot of extra money. In their eyes, the $65,000 that she made a year was more than enough money for a single woman living alone.

Juliet knew that it was a good salary; it was more than her parents ever made when they were raising a family. The problem was that she took out $180,000 worth of loans to finish vet school.

When she did it, she knew that it would take a while to pay back, but she never actually did the math. The interest rates were so high that for her first year out of school, her entire payment went towards interest. She now put half of her wages every month into the loans.

Though they never said anything, she worried that her parents thought it was a mistake that she didn't leave the clinic and go somewhere else for more money.

She couldn't imagine doing that though, and it would break her heart to hear them suggest it. It meant everything to her that she could relieve stress for people who couldn't afford their pet's emergency.

Juliet knew first hand what it was like to lose a beloved pet and be helpless to save them. A lot of the dogs that she took care of reminded her of her childhood dog Ruthie, who all of a sudden came down sick with cancer. And a lot of families looked just like hers.

For the rest of dinner, her parents were annoyingly united. They went back and forth discussing the new car that Juliet should buy. Her dad thought she would get the best use out of a pickup truck, while her mom wanted her to get a whimsical convertible.

"Mom, how many months of the year am I going to use a convertible in Michigan?"

"Who said you have to use it in Michigan?" she said. "Why don't you go and spend the winter months in Florida and take care of some animals there? You know what, we'll join you!"

Both of her parents burst into giggles.

"Ha ha, very funny," Juliet said. "I don't want to live in Florida. I like it here. And I definitely don't want a convertible. I just want a basic car that drives."

"Well, what about a Hummer?" Her dad said. "I always thought you'd look good in one of those."

"No! That's totally impractical. Dad, when I get back from my trip, can you help me buy a car at auction – "

He interrupted her. "Oh come on! You're really going to buy some banged up car that got destroyed in a crash? Why not get something new for once? It'll be the first new car any of us have ever seen."

Juliet shook her head. "I don't want a new car. I don't *need* a new car. It's a waste of money."

"You didn't go to school for all those years – "

Juliet felt her blood pressure rising. "You know that I didn't go to school so I could buy a fancy car."

Her mom waved a hand. "I still think you could afford to pay less on those loans so that you could live a little. You're only young once you know."

Juliet closed her eyes, telling herself not to ruin the holiday over something as silly as a car. What was the point of coming home for Thanksgiving if they were just going to yell at each other?

"I know, Mom. I just don't want a new car. I don't think I'll ever want one. So Dad, will you keep an eye out for something practical?"

He nodded. "Okay sweet pea, I'll do it for you. I had a feeling we couldn't get you to budge on that."

"Thank you," she said.

"But honey, I don't know how you're going to go on this trip. Dad's car broke down last week, and I need my car to get to work."

Juliet turned to her dad. "What's wrong with your car?"

He shrugged. "Not sure. I haven't had a chance to look at it yet."

Juliet bit her lip. "Do you know anybody who would loan me their car? For a good cause?"

"I know lots of people who would, but can't," her mother answered matter-of-factly.

"Shoot. Well, how much do you think it'd cost to rent a car?"

"For a week? And driving all those miles?" Her dad set his fork down and let out a sigh. "I'd say at least $200."

"What! That can't be right." Juliet pulled out her phone and did a search to see how much a rental would cost.

"Well?" asked her mom. "How's it look?"

"Dad was wrong," said Juliet. "It's not $200. It's $350."

That wasn't going to work at all. Juliet had just enough money to pay for gas and a few very cheap motels for her trip. She could put the rental on her credit card, but she was already planning to put some expenses there, and she didn't want to end up with a big bill that she couldn't pay.

"I'm sorry honey," her mom said. "I get paid next week, I can help you out."

Juliet stood from the table and gave her mom a hug. "No, Mom, I'm an adult. I'm not going to take money from my poor, old mother."

"Who are you calling old!"

Juliet gathered some dishes. "You always refer to yourself as my 'poor old mother.' It's practically the nickname you gave yourself."

"She's not wrong," her dad commented.

"That's enough out of you," her mother snapped.

"This is my problem," said Juliet, "and I know how to solve it. It's just a very...unfortunate solution."

Juliet carried the dishes into the kitchen and pulled out her phone. She stared at it for a good minute before forcing herself to type out a text message. "How do you feel about loaning me your taxi for a week?"

James' response came just a few minutes later. "Can't do. Insurance won't cover you in an accident."

"You have to be kidding me," she muttered. He could afford to buy ten brand-new cars even if she wrecked whatever fancy thing he was driving.

"Is it good in the snow, or is it some impractical rich person car?"

"Four-wheel-drive," was his response.

Juliet set her phone down and rubbed her hand over her eyes. On the one hand, spending any time with her ex-boyfriend seemed like a cruel punishment. On the other hand, she would do anything to win this contest. Even if it meant dealing with James Balin.

She still couldn't get herself to send him a message. She started washing dishes when he texted her again.

"I'll pay for gas, you pay for snacks?"

Juliet laughed. He used to say that when he wanted to convince her to take a trip somewhere. Then he found a way to pay for the snacks, too. If he was trying to be cute, he needed to stop.

"I can pay for everything myself, thank you. Can you pick me up tomorrow at 10?"

He responded instantly. "I would be honored."

She rolled her eyes and went back to washing the dishes. If he was enough of a sucker to drive her around for the next week, so be it. She didn't owe him anything. All that mattered was winning the contest and saving the clinic. That's what she would stay focused on.

Chapter 4

On Friday morning, James got up early to prepare for the road trip. He wasn't sure how many stops or cities Juliet needed to travel to, but he was hopeful that she would be agreeable to using him as a chauffeur for the entire trip.

In order to entice her to keep using his free taxi service, he did a couple of things. First, he made sure to wash and vacuum the car. Then he went to the grocery store and filled a cooler with all of her old favorite snacks – Combos, Doritos, peanut butter filled pretzels, and teriyaki beef jerky. As he loaded it into the car, he realized his dad would scold him for putting a cooler on the leather seats.

Good.

He also bought 24 bottles of ginger ale. He hoped it was still her favorite. He would use any and every trick to make her want to hang out with him.

James pulled up to Juliet's parents' house five minutes early. His stomach was unsteady. He knew that she wouldn't like his flashy Porsche; unlike the girls he met in the city, Juliet wasn't interested in cars, private jets or his six million dollar condo in Manhattan.

James himself wasn't terribly into these things, either; it all sort of fell into his lap. It was expected of him – well, expected of someone in his position. The company paid for his condo and car so that if he needed to entertain an investor, he looked like he had money. It all felt fake, and he knew that Juliet would see it and disapprove.

After taking a deep breath, he got out of the car, walked up to the front steps, and knocked. After some yelling, the front door opened.

"James! It's so wonderful to see you," said Mrs. McCarron. "Please come in."

"There's no need," bellowed Juliet's voice from inside the house. "I'll be down in a second."

Mr. McCarron emerged from the side room and stepped past his wife. "Is that what I think it is?"

"Yes sir," James said with a nod. "That's a Porsche Panamera Turbo Executive."

"Do not start talking about cars," Mrs. McCarron said with a sigh, "or I'll shut you both outside."

"You promise?" Mr. McCarron flashed a mischievous grin. "Mind if I take a look?"

James pulled the keys out of his pocket. "Of course not, go right ahead."

They were seated side-by-side in the front seats when Juliet came out with a duffel bag.

"I didn't know you were coming along Dad," she said.

He ran his hand along the center console. "I wish I was."

James leapt from his seat. "May I take your bag?"

"No, thank you. I'll just put it in the back."

James opened the back door for her and she threw the bag in.

"Did you fill the back seat with this cooler and a bunch of drinks so I couldn't sit back here? I thought I was being chauffeured around?"

James suppressed a smile. "Of course not. You can sit back with your snacks if you prefer. You'll notice that the only drink I've brought is ginger ale, and the cooler is stocked to your liking."

She lifted the lid of the cooler. "I thought I was supposed to pay for snacks? And why do a bunch of chips and pretzels need to be in a cooler? Is that what you do in New York?"

Her urge to make fun of him overruled her desire not to speak to him. That was a good sign. "No, I just didn't want all the snacks to get smashed by the drinks."

"I see." She crossed her arms and shot a disapproving look toward the front of the car. "Alright Dad, we've got to get going."

"No," he protested. "I didn't take it for a drive yet."

"They don't have time for that!" Mrs. McCarron yelled from the front door. "Get back inside, you're going to catch pneumonia!"

"This seat is heated!" Mr. McCarron yelled back. "You don't catch pneumonia on a heated seat!"

"Dad," Juliet said, "the car isn't even on. I think you're imagining things."

"I made sure to heat the seats on my way over," interjected James sheepishly.

"So it will be your fault when he catches pneumonia."

"I'm not going to catch pneumonia," Mr. McCarron protested.

Juliet got into the passenger seat next to him and buckled her seatbelt. She gave her dad a kiss on the cheek.

"Daddy, I've got a date with a parrot."

"I know, I know. Have a good trip."

He got out of the car. James thought they were going to shake hands, but instead, Mr. McCarron nodded once at him and said, "Drive safe."

"Will do," said James, returning an awkward nod. He got into the driver's seat and closed the door.

Juliet cleared her throat. "Would it be okay if we stopped in Lansing so I could pick up a few more things from my apartment?"

"Sure, that works for me." James wanted to ask if that meant that he'd be driving her past Ann Arbor, but he didn't want to spoil the moment. He had a week's worth of clothes in the trunk, because he figured it was better to be safe than sorry.

"Do you want to put your address into the GPS?" he asked.

She responded without looking at him. "No, when we get to Lansing I'll just tell you where to go."

"Okay." He stole a glance at her – her cheeks were slightly pink from the cold. She was so pretty. He reminded himself not to stare. "Is there anything that you want to listen to? I've got lots of music, a few comedy shows, the news..."

Juliet shook her head. "No, I'm fine. I have my own stuff."

She pulled out a set of headphones and placed them into her ears.

James did not plan for that. While he knew he'd have to do most of the talking, he didn't expect her to come prepared to fully ignore him.

He put on some quiet music, hoping that she might change her mind. After half an hour, she hadn't, but they were coming up on the Lansing exit and she had to start giving directions to him. He had an idea.

Just before he took the exit for Lansing, he put on a new comedy special from Jim Gaffigan. Juliet always loved him – they even went to one of his shows back when they were still dating.

Juliet finally removed her headphones. "Turn right here and go straight for about a mile."

"Okay."

She was about to speak again when she cocked her head to the side. "Is this new? From Jim Gaffigan?"

James nodded.

She bit her lip, listening to a joke about pizza with vegetables on top. She let out a chuckle.

Bingo. Good old Jim Gaffigan.

They got to her place quickly and James pulled into a parking spot behind the apartment building.

"You can stay here, I'll be quick," she said.

He was already unbuckling his seatbelt. "And miss the chance to see where you live? Never."

"Why do you need to see where I live?"

"Because," he said slowly, "I need to meet all of your pets so I can feel jealous that I don't have any."

"I don't have any pets," she said, grabbing her bag from the backseat.

"What? Why not? What kind of vet doesn't have pets?"

"Just stay here, please?"

James settled back into his seat and decided that it was best not to push his luck. Maybe her apartment was really messy and she didn't want him to see it.

Or maybe there were pictures of her boyfriend all over the place. He hadn't found a way to ask her if she was dating someone. It would be a little obvious to just blurt out, "So what's your boyfriends name?" Though that's exactly what he wanted to do.

Juliet disappeared into the building. James waited for about ten minutes until she reappeared again with a slightly larger bag.

Before she could get back to the car, an older man approached her. James couldn't make out what he was saying, but he could hear the increasing volume of the man's voice. Was he an aggressive panhandler or something?

James got out of the car and approached them. He could just make out what Juliet was saying.

"I know, and I'm working on it."

"You work on it, and I'll work on evicting you," the man said.

James approached them. The man had a thick accent – it appeared that the homeless population in Michigan was quite diverse. "Is everything okay over here?"

"Yes, it's fine, let's go," Juliet said.

The man turned to him. "Oh it's Mr. Fancy Car! Are you her boyfriend? You should give her some money so she can pay her rent."

James looked the man up and down. It was freezing outside, yet he'd run outside wearing just a thin t-shirt. His chest hair was sticking out, tangled in a gold chain. James felt a flash of embarrassment that he assumed this man was homeless. Though the guy was behaving like a jerk.

James raised an eyebrow. "If I were her boyfriend – "

Juliet cut him off. "I don't need a *boyfriend* to pay my rent. You'll get your money, calm down."

The man threw his arms up. "You better get somebody to pay it before I kick you out!"

"Hey!" James turned to face him. "You don't talk to her like that."

Juliet had her hand on the car door handle. "It's okay, let's get going."

He stared the man down. "I'm serious. Watch it buddy."

"Or what?"

"Or I'll get the best lawyer in Michigan to drag you through two years of eviction hearings."

The man stared at him, clearly weighing if he wanted to continue the argument. After a moment, he walked away, muttering to himself.

Juliet pulled the car door open and took a seat. James followed.

Once they were back inside, he asked, "What was that all about?"

"Nothing. My landlord's not the nicest guy."

Her cheeks looked flushed, and James knew that it wasn't solely from being outside. He decided to drop it.

"Are you ready for some more Jim Gaffigan?" he asked with a smile.

For the first time, she smiled at him. "Yeah, I think so."

James pressed play and put the car into drive. He tried to hide the grin on his face – she was finally speaking to him. First problem solved.

Now all he had to do was drive around and not cause any trouble. How hard could that be?

Chapter 5

Though she would never admit it, the seats in James' Porsche were unbelievably comfortable. The ride was really smooth too, despite the roads being littered with potholes.

She tried to listen to the comedy and relax, but it was tough to get over the mortifying shame that James heard her landlord yell at her. It was true that she was overdue on rent – when she found out that the clinic was in trouble, she elected to forgo half of her salary for two months so they could keep their doors open longer.

She didn't think it'd be a problem since she didn't live extravagantly, but her student loans took the bulk of her pay and she was left with very little money at the end of the month. The past month was especially tight. She had to get a cavity filled, and that wasn't cheap. Plus, she then blew two tires in a pot hole and had to replace them. She made a mental note to sell the tires off of her car before it was officially totaled.

Rent was often last on her priority list. Her landlord wasn't the nicest man, so it was easier for her to justify.

Last winter, he left their entire apartment building without heat for two weeks. Juliet threatened to report him to the authorities, and when he scoffed at her, she did just that.

Unfortunately, it was really hard to figure out who dealt with that sort of thing. She reported it to the health department, and they said that it wasn't their issue to address. She called the non-emergency police number, and they couldn't do anything but advised that she could contact a lawyer. By the time she figured out where to report it, the heat was back on.

Ever since then, she didn't feel all that bad about being late on the rent. He was the worst landlord she'd ever had.

The heat from the car seats warmed her and she felt her muscles relax. At least James had the decency not to ask questions about what was going on. He was good like that – he knew when she was embarrassed and knew not to make it worse.

That hadn't changed. Juliet pretended to look at the center console and stole a glance at him. He didn't look different, either. He still cut his hair the same way – she called it the "lazy buzzcut," because he did it himself in the bathroom. Or at least he used to. He didn't need a $100 haircut – he was *gorgeous.* He had these piercing blue eyes that disarmed Juliet – she'd get distracted in arguments by how pretty they were. That might be the only thing that was a bit different – he seemed to have bags under his eyes now. Somehow it still worked with the rugged stubble on his face.

She made herself face forward again so she wouldn't get caught looking; there was no need for him to think that she still liked him or anything. It was very odd that he showed up out of the blue and was so willing to help her. He must be up to something; she just couldn't figure out what it was. Did it have to do with his dad's business? Maybe he was spying on the other drug company?

That didn't make sense. He couldn't have known that she was going to enter this contest. And he didn't know that her car was going to break down.

Or did he?

No – James was self-absorbed, but he wasn't a monster. He wouldn't sabotage her car or risk hurting her. She couldn't figure out what he wanted, though, and it made her feel on edge.

After 45 minutes, the comedy special was over. Juliet's cheeks hurt from laughing.

"What do you want to listen to next?" asked James.

"I don't know," she said.

When she mentally prepared to spend hours in the car with her ex-boyfriend, for some reason she didn't think he'd want to talk so much. Although...the more they talked, the more likely she'd find out what he was after.

"I've got a new album from Adele," he offered.

"I didn't take you as an Adele fan."

"Excuse me," he said, throwing up a hand. "Literally one of her biggest fans. I got to see her live in London, she was incredible."

"Ooh," she cooed. "In London, aren't you fancy? Did you pay for a private performance? On your yacht?"

He glanced at her, eyes narrowed. "Is that what you think I do all day? Hang out on a yacht?"

"Yes," she said.

"Don't be ridiculous, I only use the yacht to travel to my private islands."

"What! When did you get private islands?"

He laughed. "I'm kidding. I don't have any yachts or islands. That's for people with free time."

"You seem to have a lot of free time this week."

"I'm taking some time off. So who are we seeing first? The bird?"

He changed the subject. Interesting. "Yeah. His name is Deno. He's an African Grey Parrot."

"They gave this cancer drug to a little bird? How did they even know how much to give him?"

Juliet smiled. "Yes, they give cancer drugs to birds; he was relatively young when he got the cancer. I think he was ten years old, and normally he'd have at least another fifty years to live. Dosing is a problem that we run into as veterinarians. Sometimes we know doses for dogs and cats. Other times we have to make things up for parrots, jaguars..."

"Yeah, I remember the vet from the zoo saying that. They had to base their drug dosing for the lions off of studies in house cats."

"When did you talk to a veterinarian who worked at a zoo?"

"I have my secrets," he said with a half smile. "What's this drug called? And how does it work?"

Juliet always loved that half smile – it made him look boyish and mischievous. She turned her head to look out of the window, there was no need to get caught up in his charm.

"It's called barkcizumab and it's a monoclonal antibody."

"That sounds very impressive, but confusing. You do remember how we met, right? That I had to pay you to tutor me in biology?"

Of course she remembered. Why was he bringing this stuff up?

"Basically it attaches to cancer cells and makes them self-destruct. It's really amazing, because it works for a few different kinds of cancer. It can treat skin cancer, lymphoma, even bone cancer."

"Bark-sizzle-abs?"

"Bark-sizz-oo-mab. The brand name is Delicaid. That's a lot easier to say."

"Where do they come up with this stuff?"

"Delicaid is based on 'deliciolum,' the Latin word meaning pet, or darling."

He made a face like he was impressed. "Oh. That's pretty cool."

Juliet suddenly felt embarrassed that she nerded out so much about the drug. "Let's hear that new Adele album?"

They arrived at Deno's owner's house about an hour early. Juliet fully expected James to be late, so she fibbed about what time he needed to pick her up that morning. Luckily, Deno's owner said that she was ready for them.

"I only had two students show up to my office hours today," she said as she welcomed them into her house. "Most of the students went home for Thanksgiving, but I always want to be here for the ones who might need a little extra help."

"Do you teach at the university?" asked James.

"Yes," she replied. "Mathematics. I also do research on the mathematical theory of elasticity."

"Oh, how interesting," James replied.

Juliet had to bite her lip not to smile. James was completely out of his element, but the salesman in him required that he pretended to know what was going on.

"Hi Dr. Wisniewski, it's so nice to meet you. I'm Juliet."

"Please, call me Rose."

James offered his hand. "Hi, I'm James."

Juliet pulled the camera out of its bag. "Thank you so much for agreeing to be part of the video."

"Oh, it's my pleasure! How do you want to do this?"

Juliet paused. As excited as she was to get all of these videos, she didn't plan the best way to do them. "Would we be able to ask you some questions, maybe with Deno sitting with you?"

Rose put her hands on her hips. "I have a feeling that Deno is going to be very afraid of that camera. He doesn't like new things."

"Oh, of course. How about we get some interview questions from you, and later get some footage of him from afar?"

"That sounds good."

Rose insisted on first fetching some refreshments. When she was out of earshot, James leaned in and whispered in Juliet's ear. "We definitely need a lot more footage of that bird than we do of her talking."

"How do you know? I'm sure people will want to hear what she has to say."

"Yeah, but don't you think we'd want to have most of it as a voiceover while on the screen there's a video of a super adorable cancer fighting bird?"

Juliet sighed. She couldn't really argue against that, but she didn't want to scare the poor bird. "We'll see what we can do. African Grey Parrots are really smart and really sensitive. I don't want to do anything that will upset him."

James seemed unsatisfied with that, but he didn't say anything else. Over the next hour, they collected footage of Rose talking about Deno's diagnosis and treatment.

Juliet didn't know the full story until then – apparently, Deno developed squamous cell carcinoma on the skin of his leg. It was an unusual case, and Rose was desperate to save him. After three doses of Delicaid, Deno was cured. That was four years ago, and Rose couldn't be happier. Juliet teared up as she listened.

They then took some footage of Deno in his cage from afar. Unfortunately, it didn't look great. If they got too close to the cage, he started to make loud, shrill noises like a police siren or a smoke detector.

"That's how you know he doesn't like what you're doing," said Rose. "But he might be a bit more agreeable if I let him out of his cage."

"Hold on a second," said James. "Does he fly?"

Rose laughed. "He does. Are you afraid of a little bird?"

"Absolutely. Didn't you know that Steve Irwin once said he feared parrots more than any other animal?"

Both Juliet and Rose burst into laughter.

"Don't be a baby," said Rose. "But don't let him land in your hair."

Juliet couldn't tell if she was kidding, but she decided it was better not to ask.

Juliet turned to James. "If you're really afraid, you should probably leave. I don't want you to scare him."

"I'm not going to leave," he said, lowering his voice. "I'm just saying parrots are like small dragons."

Juliet handed him the camera. "Well, here. If you're holding the camera, he probably won't come near you because he's afraid of it. Just make sure to get a lot of good shots of him."

A moment later, Rose came into the room with Deno resting on her hand. He eyed the camera suspiciously, but didn't make any loud noises. Juliet decided that was a good sign.

"What's that?" Rose asked Deno in a high voice.

He didn't answer and she repeated herself. Juliet looked at James to make sure that he was recording. He was.

After a moment of silence, Deno spoke. "Who's there? Hello?"

James and Juliet giggled. They tried to quiet down so it wouldn't ruin the video, but then Deno let out a chuckle. This sent them into uncontrollable laughter.

"Oh yes," said Rose. "He likes to laugh at people. He also can mimic a cough frighteningly well. I once called my vet in a panic thinking that he had pneumonia."

Juliet laughed. "I bet I know what he told you."

"Yeah! That parrots don't cough!" said Rose, shaking her head. "He really scared me because it sounded so awful."

The next two things happened almost at once. James took a step towards Deno, which spooked him and caused him to take flight. At the same moment, the front door opened as Rose's husband walked in the door. He didn't have a chance to react to the parrot flying directly at him.

He could only stand with his mouth open as Deno flew over his shoulder, straight through the door and into the cold Michigan sky.

Chapter 6

The parrot was gone. He was just *gone*!

James dropped the camera to his side. Was it *his* fault? No – he didn't do anything. It was the guy who opened the door. Definitely his fault.

"Okay, remain calm. Everyone outside, we need to scan the trees so we can find where he landed." Juliet nodded encouragingly and headed for the door.

Rose, mouth open, ran outside after Juliet.

James looked at the man who opened the door. His hand was still on the handle and he stood with a sheepish look on his face. Clearly this was Rose's husband, and he knew that he messed up.

"Shall we?" asked James.

He nodded. "We gotta find that bird."

They hurried outside to join Rose and Juliet. Unfortunately, the house was surrounded by tall trees. He could've gone anywhere. James looked up and down the bare branches for a glimpse of Deno – his gray feathers would be hard to see, but his red tail would make him stick out.

"Keep yelling his name, it will help him find his way back to you," said Juliet.

"Why isn't he answering? He could be a mile away!" said Rose, panic rising in her voice.

"It may be a good sign, actually," responded Juliet. "If he's being quiet, it might be because he can see you and he feels safe. Parrots don't often fly far when they're spooked."

Rose nodded and continued calling his name.

"I'll go around back and look for him," James announced to no one, as neither Juliet nor Rose acknowledged him. He went to the back of the house, disappointed to find a thick forest of trees.

Again he squinted, searching for that red tail, but saw nothing. His vision wasn't the best. After a few minutes with no success, it dawned on him that he could use the video camera to zoom in on the trees.

He took a few minutes and scanned every inch of the backyard using the camera. There was nothing, and he decided to go back out to the front to try the trick there.

He slowly made his way around the side of the house, scanning the branches and evergreen trees. At one point he spotted the red plumes of a cardinal. His heart leapt when he first saw him, but quickly fell when he realized that it was the wrong bird.

The cardinal was difficult to ignore, though, peeping wildly and jumping from twig to twig. James took the video camera and zoomed in more closely on the area.

Bingo.

Deno sat ten feet above the agitated cardinal. From his vantage point, Deno could easily see Rose, who continued frantically calling for him in the front yard.

"Hey! Everyone! I found him." James waited for a moment, but they hadn't heard him. He didn't want to lose sight of Deno, so he carefully pulled out his cell phone and called Juliet.

She answered the phone with a hushed voice. "Why are you calling me right now?"

"I found him. Come over to the side of the house."

Juliet swiftly made her way over, Rose following behind. James did not take his eyes off of Deno.

"See?" he said, pointing up at the tree. "He's right there. He looks all cozy. And there's a really angry cardinal beneath him."

"Deno! Come here sweetie. Come to my hand." Rose outstretched her arm expectantly. Deno turned his head to get a better look at her, but he didn't budge.

Juliet frowned. "This might be tough. Like I said, since he can see you, he might feel safe. And often times, they might fly really high when they're spooked, but then have no idea how to get down."

"It's so cold and it'll be dark in a few hours," said Rose. "We have to get him down soon, or something might eat him!"

The cardinal seems like he's pretty close to eating him, thought James. He didn't have any insight to offer, so he kept his mouth shut.

Juliet spoke up again in a hushed tone. "I used to work at a wildlife sanctuary, and we had a free-flight show with a couple of falcons. Every once in a while, they would fly off, but we always got them back. I don't want you to worry, okay?"

Rose nodded, her lips thin and white with pressure.

"I'd like to try bringing his cage outside. He may feel attracted to it, especially if it has some of his favorite toys."

"Okay," Rose said slowly. "Should I...?"

"No," said Juliet. "Maybe your husband could go and get it?"

"I'm on it!" he said, turning to run into the house.

James felt bad for the man. He'd probably be sleeping outside under that tree tonight.

Juliet turned to James. "I think you should back away and get out of sight. He doesn't know you, plus you have that camera that he doesn't like."

James nodded. "Okay, but I'll keep an eye on him in case he flies away again."

He walked into the backyard and planted himself behind a bush. He wanted to be helpful; it just so happened that he was most helpful while squatting in a bush.

Rose's husband came out and carefully placed Deno's cage on the ground in front of Rose. Juliet backed away and joined James behind the bush.

James felt the urge to crack a joke and ease the tension. "Bet you didn't expect to go on a wild parrot chase today," he whispered.

"That's not funny," she said gruffly, not looking at him. "Keep your voice down and try not to cause any more trouble."

What? She was not going to blame this on him. "What do you mean *more* trouble? It's not my fault that he can fly and sometimes chooses to do so."

"I am not having this conversation with you right now," said Juliet before moving to another bush.

James felt extraordinarily annoyed that she would try to pin this on him. Technically everyone played a role in the parrot getting out. Rose took him out of his cage, the husband opened the door, Juliet showed up to film the bird – and sure, James had the camera, but he didn't launch at the bird with the camera or anything. It wasn't his fault that Deno didn't understand video cameras or doors!

James had a lot of time to replay Deno's escape in his head, because he had to squat behind that bush for the next hour. He had varying degrees of numbness from his hips down. Squatting was not a good position.

Rose continued calling to Deno, but he did not move, not even by an inch.

Finally, Juliet got back up and approached Rose with a new idea. "Is Deno jealous of anyone? Like maybe your husband?"

She shook her head. "No, not really."

"How about your dog? Does he get jealous when you pay attention to the dog over him?"

"No, I can't say that he does. Sometimes he'll fly over and bite his tail, but it's not when I'm paying attention to him."

Juliet frowned. "Is there anything that you can think of that you do that makes him act out to get your attention?"

Rose paused, her line of sight with Deno unbroken. "He doesn't like when I'm on the phone for too long. He'll keep repeating 'good-bye' and start making police siren noises."

"Ah," said Juliet. "Okay, here's what I want you to do. I'm going to go back and hide in the bushes so I can keep an eye on him. I want you to pull out your phone and pretend like you're having a conversation. I want you to walk away, slowly, and go back into the house."

"I can't leave him out here!" Rose protested.

"I know. But I think he's afraid of the height and afraid to come down. As long as he knows that you're nearby, he feels safe. But we can't sit here much longer, he's going to freeze. We have to get him moving."

Rose stood for a moment, considering it. Finally she agreed to try. Juliet ran back to hide. Rose's husband, who was stationed in the front yard, found himself a hiding spot as well. James made sure not to move, even though he felt like his spine was going to break.

Rose took a deep breath and pulled out her cell phone. "Hello? Hi, thanks for calling. What am I doing? Oh, you know, just trying to convince a stubborn bird to come back in the house..." She turned and started walking away.

At first, Deno didn't flinch. But then, he stooped low, trying to get a better look at Rose. He stood up really straight and stretched out his wings. He flapped a few times as though to get her attention. She kept walking.

Finally, when she was almost to the house, he let out a shrill squawk before leaping from the tree, flying directly towards Rose.

She turned and saw him coming before quickly sticking out her arm. He landed gracefully on her hand. Without another word, she darted into the house.

Chapter 7

Finally, something worked.

Juliet stood up from behind the bush. Her hands and feet were freezing, but it felt like they might finally be getting some blood flow again.

She kept telling Rose that there was nothing to worry about, though that wasn't entirely true. A lot could have gone wrong and sent Deno flying into the distance never to be seen again. Juliet took a deep breath – thank goodness that didn't happen.

Rose's husband approached. "Thank you so much, I don't know what we would've done without you."

Juliet cringed. "If we hadn't come in the first place, this never would've happened. I'm so sorry. We'll go now."

"No." He shook his head. "Please, come inside and warm up."

"I'm sure that Rose would prefer to never see us again," Juliet said, rubbing her forehead.

"Just wait here," he said. "I'll go inside and check on them and see what the mood is like."

"Appreciate it!" yelled James.

Juliet closed her eyes. As much as she needed James for a ride, she couldn't bring him along if he was going to endanger the life of every pet they met along the way. She couldn't yell at him in front of everyone, but she also didn't know how long she could keep it in. She waited until Rose's husband disappeared into the house before she turned to James.

"Could you act even *a little bit* sorry about what happened?"

"What!" he protested. "I feel really bad that the bird escaped. It's not like I *wanted* that to happen."

"But it doesn't matter to you that it happened, does it?"

"How is this my fault?"

Juliet sighed and walked away from him. "Nothing is ever your fault, is it James?"

Before he could respond, Rose's husband came back outside. "Juliet, would you mind taking a look at Deno to make sure that he's okay?"

"Of course," she said, following him to the house.

Juliet was very careful when she opened and closed the door behind her – so careful that James wasn't able to make it inside with her. She turned and gave him a dirty look through the window, motioning that he should go back to the car. He eventually relented.

She found Deno in the kitchen with his feet wrapped around the sink faucet.

"I'm running the hot water to warm him up," said Rose. "Do you think he's going to be okay? He's not supposed to be out in the cold."

Juliet slowly walked towards him. "I think so. Has he been acting normally?"

Rose nodded. "Yes, but his feet were freezing. I cut up some of his favorite fruits to see if he wants to eat."

She handed him a slice of apple. He immediately reached out to take it and started devouring it.

Juliet took a few minutes to examine him. "Even though it felt like an eternity, we weren't out there that long. He had some cover from the trees, plus he puffed up his feathers to keep himself warm. I don't see anything wrong with him and I think he's going to be okay. I'm glad that it wasn't colder today and the sun was out."

Rose let out a big sigh. "Thank goodness."

Juliet continued. "I cannot tell you how sorry I am that this happened. I will – "

Rose held up a hand to stop her. "Please, don't worry. This isn't the first time that he's gotten out. But it was the coldest and longest trip that he's had. Last time, it was my son that opened the window and scared him. This time it was my husband. These men are going to kill my bird!"

Rose and Juliet burst into laughter.

"I have to remember that trick about the phone in case he gets out again," said Rose. "That was perfect. He can't stand me being on the phone."

"Yeah," Juliet said with a smile. "That really motivated him. I'm so relieved that he flew down. And again, I'm so sorry."

Rose smiled. "Everything's okay. Can I give you some tea to warm you up?"

Juliet waved a hand. "No, thank you. We should get going."

"Alright," said Rose. "But be sure to send me the video when it's done! My Deno is going to be famous!"

"He certainly is!"

Juliet thanked her again and headed out to the car. James was there, listening to music.

"I'm guessing you don't want to listen to Adele right now?" he said.

"You guessed right. Please take me back to Lansing."

He scrunched his eyebrows together. "I thought we were going to Dayton tomorrow?"

"*We* are not going anywhere. *I'm* going home."

Even as she said the words, she knew they didn't make sense. She had no way of getting herself to Dayton, but she couldn't stand spending another minute with him.

"Oh come on," he said. "Driving back to Lansing today will take an hour. Then tomorrow, we'll have to come back this exact same way and it'll just add an hour to our time."

"You don't have to worry about it," she said. "Because from here on out, I'm going to rent a car and do the rest of this trip myself."

"Is this because of the bird?"

"What do you think?" Her voice rose. "And he's not a bird, he's a parrot!"

"He's a bird, he's a parrot, he's a little feathery dragon – whatever you want to call him," said James. "And I'm sorry. I'm sorry that he got outside and almost froze to death. I'm sorry that he almost turned into a parrot popsicle."

"That's not funny," said Juliet, even as she felt a smile tugging at the corner of her mouth.

"You're right, it wouldn't have been funny if it happened, but it didn't happen. So we can joke about it."

Juliet let out a frustrated sigh as she replayed Deno's escape in her head. "Why did you lunge at him with the camera? You knew he was afraid of it."

"I didn't *lunge* at him!"

"Yes you did. I'll play the video and show you."

James frowned. "I don't know that we need to review the evidence here."

"Yes we do, because you never admit that you're wrong."

She sat there, arms crossed, awaiting his response. This was a fight they often had when they were dating. James never fully took the blame for anything.

Finally, he spoke up.

"I'm sorry that Deno got out. I was genuinely afraid of him, but when I saw how great the footage was of him out of his cage, I got a little too excited. I admit that I stepped towards him and that spooked him into flying. Unfortunately, at that same moment, Rose's husband opened the door. It was a recipe for disaster, and yes, I played a big role. I'm very sorry that I wasn't more careful."

Juliet kept glaring at him. Was he actually apologizing? This was very unlike him. Was this a part of his ploy?

"I didn't mean for it to happen," he continued. "But you were amazing! You knew exactly what to do to save him. I'm a dunce when it comes to birds, but you saved the day. Will you please let me make it up to you?"

She shifted in her seat. "I don't know. You almost killed him!"

"Please don't make me go back to Lansing today," he pleaded.

Juliet laughed. "What's wrong with Lansing?"

"Nothing," he said. "But it's one hour in the wrong direction. How about you let me formally apologize for my role in Deno's great escape? It's getting pretty late, we can get a nice dinner, and I would happily pay for a hotel so we can start fresh from Ann Arbor in the morning."

Juliet opened her mouth to protest, but James cut her off. "Obviously we would get separate hotel rooms."

"Good," she said. "Because – "

"I know!" He flashed a smile at her. "I have a really important question for you, though."

Oh no, was this it? Was he going to ask for whatever he was after now?

"What?"

"What do you think is going to happen to Rose's husband? I mean, he's the one who actually opened the door, and I'm guessing that they're still not speaking. Should I get him a room, too?"

Juliet giggled, rubbing her face with her hands. "I do feel bad for the guy. Deno is clearly a one-woman kind of bird."

James nodded. "There's no room for the husband in that relationship."

"No, there isn't," she agreed.

"So what do you say? I admit that I'm an idiot and I'm afraid of little parrots. You can enjoy a nice dinner at a restaurant of your choice and not make me drive back to Lansing today."

It was tempting. Plus it would save them a lot of time. Even though she threatened to rent a car, her credit card was almost maxed out, so that wasn't a real option. If she wanted to make this video and potentially save the clinic, James was her best bet.

At least he admitted that he messed up, which James from five years ago never would've done.

She squinted at him. "Can we get Chinese food?"

"I thought you'd never ask."

Juliet found a nearby restaurant online and James started driving. She still didn't know what he was up to, but at least he was being nice.

There was no harm in being civil with him. For now.

Chapter 8

They made it to the restaurant in fifteen minutes. James was glad to see that Juliet's mood improved; he thought that he was about to get the boot there for a minute.

He didn't know what saved it – was it the thought of dinner, or a warm bed to sleep in? Or was it the fact that he took the blame for his role in Deno's escape? Whatever it was, James was happy. He just got her to start speaking to him. He needed more than one day to get her to fall in love with him again.

The restaurant was packed and buzzing with activity. They were seated at a high table right in the middle of all the action. It made it a bit hard to talk, but James was undeterred.

He squared himself away in his seat. "Alright, I'm going to guess what you're going to order."

"I'd like to see you try." Juliet crossed her arms.

James smiled. He liked the challenge – and he liked to think he still knew Juliet pretty well.

"What do I get if I'm right?"

"You get to brag that you were right about something."

"Fair enough." He picked up the menu and scanned the options. On second thought, this might not be the best restaurant for this game. The menu had five pages of stuff.

"Are you ready?" she asked.

He flipped back a page and studied a few options before making his decision. "Yes. You're going to order...the Amazing Chicken."

"Nope."

He narrowed his eyes. "How do I know that you didn't just change your mind last minute so that I couldn't be right?"

"Look at your phone," she said.

James pulled his cell phone out of his pocket. There was a text from her that read, "Szechuan tofu."

He shook his head. "When did you go vegetarian?"

She laughed. "I'm not vegetarian, I just try to eat tofu sometimes. I...feel bad for the chickens."

"What about cows?"

"Definitely feel bad about cows, too." She cleared her throat. "I know what you're going to order."

"Oh yeah? Try me."

"First text me so you can't cheat."

He typed out his meal and hit send.

Juliet didn't break eye contact. "Pad Thai."

"How did you know that?" he exclaimed.

She laughed. "You always order that. I had a feeling you hadn't changed."

He crossed his arms. "What do you mean? You think I haven't changed at all in the last five years?"

"Honestly?" She sat back and studied him for a moment. "No."

He opened his mouth in mock outrage. "I resent that. I'll have you know that I memorized the opening lines to Law and Order SVU, plus my doctor said I have arthritis in my right knee. Those are some big changes if I do say so myself."

"Sure," she said. "And you're still ordering Pad Thai everywhere you go."

"What's wrong with Pad Thai? It's a great meal."

"Nothing," she said. "You just never get to experience anything new."

"What's so great about new things? I usually work at least 60 hours a week. If I have the chance to relax and have a nice dinner, I can't risk ordering something weird. My life is too tumultuous to risk something like that."

She laughed heartily. "Seriously?"

"Alright," he said, "I'm going to order something different today."

"Like what?"

"Well," he reopened the menu. "I'm not going to tell you so that you can't make fun of me."

"Okay."

She looked away at her cell phone. James had a hard time focusing on the menu; he kept staring at her. How he missed that smile all of this time. James would happily try a new meal if it would show her that he was different than before.

They placed their orders, James getting something with scallops in it, and their food came out surprisingly quickly.

"Do you think they just have it ready back there?" asked James. "Do people only order like three revolving things?"

"If the restaurant patrons are anything like you, then yes," she replied.

They were both hungry and finished their meals quickly. James thought his choice was pretty good, but not as good as the Pad Thai would've been. He decided not to mention that to her.

He managed to pay for the tab when she went to use the restroom. Even though he didn't know how much money he had in his bank account, he knew that it was more than she had in hers. She was on another level, getting verbally attacked by her landlord. The least he could do was pay for things here and there.

When she returned, he excused himself to use the restroom. Really what he wanted to do was call a hotel and book two rooms under his name before she could protest.

He knew that she wouldn't like that he paid for dinner and then paid for the hotel rooms, but this was part of his apology, so it had to be allowed.

He had to break the news to her when he got back to the table. She was already sitting there, arms crossed.

"You didn't have to pay for my meal," she said. "This isn't a date, you know."

He put his hands up, as if to surrender. "Yes, don't attack! I know this isn't a date, but this is my apology for scaring the parrot into a near death experience. Remember?"

She gave a begrudging shrug.

"And because I'm the one who doesn't want to drive back to Lansing, I also took the liberty to book our rooms at The Tiffany Suites."

"James!" she said. "That place is crazy expensive."

"Again," he said with a wince, "this is part of my apology. I travel a lot for work, actually I travel most weeks during the year. So I have a lot of rewards points with them. The rooms were practically free. And you're going to have a really comfortable bed, and everything in the mini fridge is complementary."

This piqued her interest. "Really? They never do that. It's always like six dollars for a candy bar."

"This place is the best. Trust me."

She sighed. "Alright. After eating all that food, I feel like I'm going to fall asleep immediately."

"Let's get going then."

The hotel was about twenty minutes away, and when they got there, their rooms were ready. James walked her to her door.

"Alright, so, what time do we leave tomorrow?" he asked.

"Well…" She looked up, and counted on her fingers. "We have four owners to meet, and the middle two are flexible on time. It's going to be an all day thing, though, to get to all of them. I was hoping we could leave at eight?"

"You got it," he said. He had to resist the urge to give her a hug. He knew she wouldn't appreciate that. "Okay, well, if you need anything, let me know. I'm just across the hall."

She opened her door. "Thanks. And thank you for dinner."

"It was my pleasure. If you'll excuse me, I'm going to carefully open my door and make sure there are no parrots in there waiting to fly out."

She chuckled. "Okay James. Have a good night."

He scolded himself for making a stupid joke. James stayed up for another hour in case she needed something, but she didn't text him or knock on the door, so he finally got in bed and went to sleep.

He set an alarm for seven the next morning so he had enough time to shower. While showering, room service dropped off breakfast. Since he stayed at this hotel chain all the time for work, he was a Gold Star member, so breakfast was included with every room.

He forgot about this until he got an angry text from Juliet that morning. "Seriously? You don't have to pay for all of my food, I'm not a pauper!"

"I'm sorry! I forgot to tell you that breakfast is complementary. I swear, I didn't do this!"

She sent back a smiley face with the word "Whoops!"

He needed to be careful. As much as he wanted to shower her with good food and comfortable hotel rooms, Juliet didn't like money being spent on her.

It was always a tense topic when they were dating. James grew up with a lot of money. His father was never around since he worked so much, but James never wanted for anything. Nothing material, at least.

He had a nice car and nice clothes. His dad paid for all of the fees and gear for football, but rarely came to any of the games.

Money never mattered to James. True, he never had to live without it, but because of that, it was never important to him. If he offered to take Juliet to a nice dinner when they were dating, or suggested a trip for a long weekend, she acted strange. She didn't want him to pay for her, but she also didn't have the money herself and would never say that.

He never thought of it as "his" money; he always thought they were going to get married, so it was as good as her money anyway. Juliet didn't think like that. She never wanted to be seen as a free-loader.

He made a mental note to be more mindful of that for the rest of the trip.

They got on the road promptly at 8:05. It was a three hour drive to their first stop. James came prepared; he picked out five different podcasts that they could listen to, and downloaded ten new albums of artists he thought she'd like. He let Juliet take her pick of what to listen to, and the drive flew by.

Their first stop was with a man named Stephen. His cat Mr. Wigglesworth took Delicaid for treatment of lymphoma. He was thrilled to be in the video, and even more thrilled that his beloved cat was now three years cancer free.

"It's really incredible," said James.

Stephen beamed. "It really is. I don't know what I would've done without her."

James turned to look at Juliet and realized that she had tears in her eyes. He changed the topic, stooping down to pet Mr. Wigglesworth.

"Do you know what breed he is?" asked James.

Stephen shook his head. "No idea. I got him from the shelter when he was a kitten."

Mr. Wigglesworth leaned into James, purring loudly. "I think he likes me!"

"He's an extremely friendly cat," said Stephen, grin unbroken. "The girls at the vet clinic said they'd carry Wiggles around like a baby, and he'd just throw his paws back and purr."

"I believe it," James replied. Mr. Wigglesworth was absolutely adorable. They chatted for a few more minutes, but sadly had to get on to their next stop.

"Shall we head out?" he asked Juliet.

She nodded. "Let's go."

It took them five hours to get through the next three stops. The second stop was for a cat who had kidney cancer, and the third and fourth stops were for dogs that had lymphoma. All the filming went well, and the owners were delighted to share their stories. All of them were endlessly grateful to the company for making a drug that saved their beloved pets.

James realized that this video was going to be *very* good advertising for the company; even if they hired actors to make a commercial, it would not be nearly as good or as touching as these true stories.

They got a quick dinner that evening at Chipotle. Juliet insisted on paying, and James let her. He didn't want to make her feel "like a pauper."

They made their way back to the car after dinner, and Juliet gave him Greg's address – he lived just outside of Dayton in Springboro and offered to let them spend the night.

He put the address into the GPS before turning to her. "Can I request one thing?"

She raised an eyebrow. "It depends what that is."

"I need you to tell me that I did a better job today. I didn't almost kill any of the cancer surviving pets."

Juliet burst into laughter, hiding her face in her hands. She had such a great laugh. James felt like his soul expanded every time he heard it.

Finally, she said, "James, you did a very good job not killing any of the pets today."

He smiled broadly. "Thanks, that means a lot."

"You're welcome."

He put the car into drive. With a few more days, he might win her over after all.

Chapter 9

It didn't take long to get to Greg's place, and Juliet was glad, because the day's activities really wore her out. James insisted on carrying her bag inside for her, so Juliet pushed the door open for him.

Greg was waiting for them and greeted them in the doorway. "Welcome to my humble abode!"

Juliet hugged him. "Hey! Thank you so much for hosting us."

"It's my pleasure." Greg shook James' hand. "Kerry was sorry she couldn't be here, she had to cover a flight for a friend, so she's in Paris until tomorrow. "

"Kerry? Kerry Walsh?" James asked.

Greg nodded. "The one and only. Except she made the mistake of marrying me, so now she's Kerry Boulder."

"Wow," said James. "And she's a...flight attendant?"

"She's a pilot," said Greg.

"Oh, sorry. Shouldn't have assumed."

Juliet resisted the urge to call him out on being sexist.

"You guys were high school sweethearts, right?" asked James.

Juliet couldn't stop herself this time. "Yes James, some people are capable of long-term loving relationships."

"Ah, yes," James said without missing a beat. "It's good that there's still that kind of beauty in the world. It's kinda like two old friends taking a road trip together for a good cause."

Juliet made a point to ignore him and instead take her bag from his hand.

Greg cracked a smile. "Let me show you to your rooms. I know you've had a busy day."

"That would be great, thank you," said Juliet.

Greg led them upstairs. Juliet got her favorite room in the house – it had a big window that overlooked the vast wooded space behind Greg's yard. It was so peaceful that it made her feel like she was on vacation.

"Alright," said Greg, "how about you give me the camera so I can upload the new footage and tinker with it? Do you want to take a shower or anything?"

Juliet was covered in dog and cat fur. "That sounds perfect. Unless – did you want to shower first, James?"

He shook his head. "No, go right ahead. I'll give Greg some context about the pets we saw."

Juliet took a hot shower and enjoyed every minute of it. It was draining to spend all day talking to new people. She'd always been more of an animal person.

It wasn't that she didn't like people, but she found animals easier to be around. She could be herself; she didn't have to try to be nicer, or more feminine, or more polite. All she had to do was treat them with respect, and they often responded in kind. With animals, she always knew what she was going to get. Even parrots were less unpredictable than people.

Right now, the most unpredictable person in her life wasn't her crazy landlord or even the panel that would pick the winner for the competition. It was James.

He was definitely up to something, but she couldn't figure out what. He hadn't dropped any hints yet. Juliet wanted him to ask questions or something – anything – yet he gave no hint of what he was after.

How could he possibly have an entire week off of work? Whenever he talked about his job, all he said was how much time he spent traveling and working. It seemed like work was his life, and it'd be unlikely that his dad would just give him a week off to have fun. Something was definitely up.

After her shower, Juliet ventured downstairs to find Greg and James at the computer.

"Hey," said Greg as she approached. "James showed me some of the highlights from today's videos. I'm going to edit what we have so far – I have some good ideas for music and graphics, too."

"That sounds great," said Juliet. "Do you have any questions for me? Like about the animals, or the drug?"

"Not yet," said Greg. "But I will soon. I'm working on a little graphic showing how the drug works. People love that stuff."

"People do love that," agreed James.

Juliet let out a sigh. "Don't let James bully you into making the video based off of what he thinks people like or don't like."

"I'm not bullying," said James with a smile. "I'm supporting. And suggesting."

"Right," she said. "Do you want to take a shower now? I know you got mud all over your jeans at our last stop."

"That was *just* mud?" He said, wide-eyed. "I was too afraid to smell it."

She rolled her eyes. "Bye James."

"Goodbye Juliet," he called as he headed towards the stairs. "Sweet dreams, don't let the bed parrots bite."

"Bed parrots," Juliet muttered to herself, shaking her head.

"That parrot did seem pretty scary," said Greg. "You can actually see him on the video – he flies directly at the camera."

Juliet groaned. "You can't use that! The escape was awful. I thought he was going to die."

"I know, I know," said Greg. "But the video is great. The best part is the little squeal that James let out."

Juliet felt a smile creeping across her face. "Like out of fear?"

"Yeah," Greg replied. "It's *so* funny. At first, I thought it was you, because it was so high-pitched. It sounds like a little girl. But it's definitely James."

Now she was interested. "Please tell me that you made him watch that."

"Oh absolutely. It was the first thing I showed him."

"And?"

"He insisted that there was a mouse offscreen that made the noise."

"Nope, no mouse," said Juliet. "Just a grown man afraid of a bird."

Greg turned back to the computer screen. "You two seem to be getting along a little better than you were before Thanksgiving."

"Don't," warned Juliet.

"What?" he said innocently. "You're speaking to him, which is an improvement. You're not being nice to him, but you *are* speaking to him."

"How am I not being nice to him?"

Greg put a hand up. "Whoa, no need to be defensive!"

"I'm not being defensive!" Juliet shot back, her voice inexplicably rising.

Greg made a face before turning back to the computer. "Sounds like a very defensive thing to say."

Juliet scolded herself for walking into Greg's teasing. "Listen, I'm trying to be civil with him, because he *is* driving me around. But I feel like he wants something – he's not doing it out of the kindness of his heart. I just don't know what that something is."

"It's probably that he's still in love with you," said Greg.

Juliet scoffed. "Yeah right."

"There are worse things, you know, than a billionaire being in love with you."

"He's not in love with me!" Juliet said with a hushed voice.

What a thing to say! And what did it matter that he was rich? Was that supposed to make her swoon? Make her want to put on makeup or flirt with him and laugh at his dumb jokes? Yeah right.

She continued. "If he were in love with me, he could have just told me that when we ran into him at the restaurant. It would've been a lot easier than having to drive me around."

Greg crossed his arms. "I don't think that would be easy at all. You're kind of intimidating."

"Alright, you clearly have your own little theory that you're not going to give up. But I'm telling you, I'm going to figure out what he wants."

"Good luck," Greg said with a smirk. "Did you know he was on the list of 30 most eligible bachelors under 30 last year?"

"I think *you're* a little in love with him," Juliet said flatly.

Greg laughed. "I'm not, I just thought you should know. It said his dad's company is worth fifteen *billion* dollars, and he's next in line to take over."

"So that's what makes him so eligible? That his daddy's rich? Wow, what a catch."

"No, that's not all," Greg said with a frown. "I don't know, you dated him. You tell me."

She looked over her shoulder to make sure that James hadn't come back. "Considering that *I* broke up with *him,* I have a different view of how great he is to date."

"He's older and wiser now," said Greg.

"Says the president of his fan club."

She wasn't going to win this argument. Greg and Aaron always liked James. When she'd broken up with James all those years ago, it was too painful to tell them what happened at first.

When she finally did tell them the full story, they reacted like she was making a big deal out of nothing. They didn't say that, of course, but it was clear that they didn't understand.

Juliet wanted to change the subject, so she asked Greg to show her some of the clips they picked out of the interviews. So far it seemed like he was doing a great job. And as much as she enjoyed hearing James squeal like a little girl as Deno flew towards him, it was not appropriate to use that clip in the video.

"How long is this supposed to be again?" asked Greg.

"Well, we need two versions," said Juliet. "One has to be less than three minutes so it can be shared more easily, like on Facebook I guess. And one needs to be less than ten minutes, but has to give more information."

Greg nodded. "Okay, no problem."

Juliet bit her lip. "I really, really appreciate you doing this."

"And I really appreciate you trying to save your clinic, so we're even. You'd better get to bed, actually."

"Why?"

"James said that you have to leave at seven tomorrow."

"What? All we're doing is driving to Louisville tomorrow. We're not even filming until Monday."

Greg sighed. "That's the thing with these lovestruck billionaires. They're always coming up with schemes."

Juliet rolled her eyes. "Alright, thank you. Good night."

"Good night!"

Juliet went upstairs and softly knocked on James' door. He didn't answer, which was awkward; it was possible that he was already sleeping.

She quietly spun around to go back to her room at the exact moment that he came around the corner. Her head collided with something firm.

"Oh my goodness, I'm so sorry!" she said.

She pulled away, realizing that the firm thing was his bare chest. He'd walked out of the bathroom wearing only a pair of jeans, and the more she told herself not to stare, the harder it was to look away.

"Are you okay?" he asked, gently placing his hands on her shoulders.

"Yes, I'm fine, are you okay?"

Stop looking at his arms. Stop looking at his arms. Were they always this muscular? Stop looking at his arms!

"Yeah, I'm fine," he said as he pulled a black T-shirt over his head. "It just seemed like you were moving quickly and hit your head pretty hard."

She made a fist and knocked twice on her head. "Nope! Hard as a rock! Or full of rocks, whatever it is!"

Juliet rushed toward her room, chiding herself for acting like such a dweeb.

"Okay!" He called from behind her. "Oh – one more thing. I've sort of planned something fun for tomorrow, so we need to leave at seven."

She nodded. "Yep, okay, that's fine. I'll see you tomorrow."

He stared at her for a moment, as though waiting for her to argue. Finally he said, "Okay, well, have a good night."

"You too!"

She closed the door and let out a sigh. What was that all about? Why was he walking around like that? Didn't he know that there were other people in the house? How did he have so much time to work out when he was allegedly constantly traveling and working? Didn't he have friends or a life outside of work and muscle building?

Whatever. None of it mattered. Juliet got ready for bed, firmly telling herself that there was only one thing that she should be thinking about during this trip.

It didn't matter how good her ex-boyfriend looked with his shirt off. It didn't even really matter what he was after. All that mattered was putting together the best video and saving the clinic. She repeated that to herself as she turned off the light.

Chapter 10

Early the next morning, James woke up and got himself ready. He was surprised that Juliet didn't try to argue with him the night before; she didn't even ask what he was planning. She must've been very distracted.

Hopefully she hadn't gotten any bad news or had disliked the video. So far they'd been pretty lucky with getting to all the pet owners on time, but they were running on a tight schedule. To meet all of these people, record enough video, and edit it all together in time for the deadline – they needed to keep being lucky.

Ten minutes to seven, he quietly knocked on the door to Juliet's bedroom. No answer.

Greg was still sleeping, so he wanted to make sure not to disturb him, but since Juliet wasn't responding, he knocked a little more loudly.

Still nothing.

In a coarse whisper, he said, "Juliet! Are you ready?"

Finally, he heard some rustling.

"Juliet?"

He could hear her coming towards him. She cracked the door and peered. "What?"

"We gotta get going."

She let out a sigh. "I think I overslept."

"Well chip-chap-chip Cinderella! It's time to go!"

She groaned. "Why do we have to get up so early? I wanted to sleep in a little bit."

"You agreed to it." He knew that she was too groggy to realize that wasn't exactly true. "Come on, we can get breakfast on the way."

"Why did you call me Cinderella?" she said, rubbing an eye.

James tried not to laugh. "Because if you don't get going soon, you're going to turn into a pumpkin."

"That's not how that works."

"It is today," he said, his whisper breaking with laughter. "Let's go!"

She shut the door. James could hear her getting things together, so he quietly went downstairs to put his bag and the camera in the car.

They were on the road twenty minutes later. That was another remarkable thing about Juliet – it never took her long to get ready. James was always so impressed by that.

"So why are you rushing me to Louisville?" asked Juliet once she was more awake.

"Do you really want to know, or would you prefer that it was a surprise?"

Juliet rubbed her forehead. "I think I'd rather know. I'm having a hard time imagining what kind of surprise you found."

"Alright then, I'll tell. We don't have anyone to actually film today, right?"

Juliet nodded. "Right. Is this surprise going to take all day?"

"Kind of." He took his phone from the center console and handed it to her. "Look at my email, there's a confirmation for our activity today."

She shot him a weary look before picking up his phone. She found it in a minute. "Ah, I see. We're going on a food tour?"

"Not just any food tour!" he said. "We'll get to see the city with an experienced tour guide, and we will get to have seven stops between breakfast, lunch, and dinner."

"Huh," she said. "That actually seems...kinda cool."

"Yeah, it'll be fun." Plus it showed that he could be adventurous with food.

She tossed his phone back into place. "We'll see. Are we going to be late? It said it starts at nine."

"No, I think we should be good," replied James confidently.

Not ten minutes later, they were stuck in standstill traffic. James regretted tempting the traffic gods with his overly confident statement.

It took some time, but eventually they got past the scene of an accident where a pickup truck flipped on its roof. After that, traffic flowed freely again.

"So all that traffic was caused by people rubbernecking," commented Juliet.

"That's right," said James, getting over to the left lane. "Now we need to make up some time so we don't miss the first breakfast."

"Oh boy," said Juliet. "I forgot how much you liked to speed."

James smiled. "Is it really speeding if your car is built to go fast?"

"Speeding is always irresponsible," said Juliet. "Unless you're driving an ambulance or something. Or you're a firefighter."

"I'd like to be a firefighter," mused James.

She scoffed. "You don't have what it takes."

He cleared his throat. "I'm not going to address that, because I need to focus on getting us to breakfast on time, but I know you don't mean it."

He didn't have to look at her – he knew that she was rolling her eyes.

With a touch of speeding, they made it to the food tour's first location only ten minutes late. There were six other people on the tour, all couples. As much as James wanted to comment on it being a couple activity, he knew that it would annoy Juliet, so he kept his mouth shut.

Their tour guide was a born-and-raised Kentuckian named Margo. At the first stop, they enjoyed French pastries and croissants, learning that Louisville was named after French King Louis XVI.

James kept shooting nervous glances at Juliet, hopeful that she would enjoy herself enough to forgive him for waking her up so early and calling her Cinderella.

By the time they got to the steamboat stop for their first lunch, he was fairly confident that he succeeded. Juliet made friends with everyone on the tour. One couple even had a cat that was treated with Delicaid.

Juliet was thrilled to hear their story, but as much as the couple wanted to be in the video, it just wasn't possible. They traveled in from Tucson, Arizona, and their beloved cat was still back in the desert.

Juliet promised to email them the final copy of the video once it was submitted to the competition. James couldn't believe how widespread the use of this drug was.

After lunch, they had a laid back bus tour that included the history of the Kentucky Derby and Mohammed Ali. James knew better than to take Juliet to an actual horse race; she could never stand to see the injuries that happened to the horses.

He knew that she would love the end of their tour. It covered the history of Kentucky Fried Chicken and ended at what was allegedly the best barbecue pit in Kentucky. They hung out at the restaurant a few hours after the tour was over, talking to some of the other couples.

By eight o'clock, everyone agreed that they were tired and ready to turn in for the night. Juliet seemed disappointed to end the experience, but she agreed it'd been a long day.

They were a few blocks away from the French bakery where they first started. James didn't know how to break it to her that he booked two rooms at another Tiffany Suites in town.

Luckily, as they walked back to the car, she said that she tried to find a hotel in the city on her phone and couldn't find anything for less than $300 a night.

"There must be some sort of an event or conference going on," she said.

"Oh, that's funny," he said lightly. "Because the Tiffany Suites always make sure that they have rooms available for Gold Star members."

She covered her face with her hands. "Of *course* they do. They wouldn't want you Gold Star members to have to feel like us regular peasants."

"That's right," he responded.

"Well," she said, looking around. "Are you still using your points for the rooms?"

"Yes," he lied. He wasn't sure how much truth there was in that. He had a lot of points – though he wasn't sure how that all worked. Embarrassingly, he never had to pay attention to that stuff. But he didn't want Juliet to know that, she would only think less of him.

"Alright, I guess it's a good option then. If you don't mind," she quickly added.

"It's my pleasure," he said. That, at least, was the truth.

Getting to the hotel was uneventful and they said their good-nights. The next morning, Juliet was not surprised by the complementary breakfast that she received at her door, and subsequently did not send James another angry text about it.

James made sure to push back the delivery time of their breakfasts to nine o'clock so Juliet finally had a chance to sleep in. They only had one stop for the day, and they didn't need to be there until eleven o'clock.

James used his free time to check out the hotel gym. He loved hotel gyms. Since he traveled so much, it was one of the few things that he could do that kept his life consistent. They were almost always empty, and almost always stocked with free water. Often there were great views as well. This hotel was no different.

He waited to knock on Juliet's door until 10:30. She opened it immediately, ready to go and fully reenergized.

"Where are we going again?" he asked. He had a hard time keeping track of their schedule. That was probably because Juliet never actually told him the schedule.

"It's a place called Ink Drop Farms. It's a horse farm – they teach riding lessons, go on trail rides, and board horses. But a few years ago, the owner and her husband decided that they wanted to start offering low cost equine therapy."

She *had* mentioned this. "Oh yeah, I remember now."

"Our patient is Snoopy. He's a quarter horse, and the first horse therapist at the farm."

"I already love him," said James.

They arrived at the farm in time to meet with Cindy, the owner. They got a great video of her walking around the farm, explaining why she and her husband Bob decided to develop the equine therapy program. Snoopy tagged along, following them.

"Bob was already a certified counselor, and we realized that there are a lot of kids who could benefit from pet therapy. But it's so expensive! We were both able to get certified pretty easily, so we can even charge insurance. But if the kid doesn't have insurance, or it's still too expensive, we offer hour-long therapy sessions at a really low rate."

James looked over at Juliet and realized that her eyes were starting to get glossy again. How did she get through the day if she got weepy so easily? She was ridiculous – but in such a lovely way. He felt his heart squeeze.

He decided that he needed to do the prompting. "What kind of kids do you see here?"

Cindy took a deep breath. "Well. We have a lot of autistic kids who really benefit from developing a relationship with the horses. We have several kids with Down Syndrome, and a handful with cerebral palsy. I wish you could include some of the testimonials from their parents."

James pet the forelock of the sleepy horse standing next to Cindy. Snoopy closed his eyes, clearly appreciating the attention.

Cindy continued. "Snoopy was the first horse that we trained. He's so gentle and he loves kids. It was devastating when we found out that he had skin cancer. The kids love him – I mean just *love* him. And we love him too." Her voice broke and she looked away.

"He seems like quite the gentleman," Juliet said, placing a gentle hand on his neck.

Cindy recovered with a smile. "He is. If it weren't for the Delicaid, I just don't know. If we lost him so young – he was only eight years old – I feel like the entire program would've fallen apart. I would've fallen apart."

Juliet pinched her lips together. "Okay, if you're going to make me cry, we're not going to get anything done."

They both started laughing. James tried to hold the camera steady.

"The Delicaid didn't only save his life. It saved ours too."

Bingo, thought James. They couldn't have gotten a better line if they wrote a script. Juliet was going to be thrilled.

Chapter 11

They got back to the car and Juliet didn't have to fight the tears any longer. At first it was just a few – but soon, she was full-on sobbing and snorting.

James stared with wide eyes. "What's wrong? I thought we got some really good stuff for the video. What didn't you like? We can go back, we still have time!"

It took her a moment to choke out a reply. "It's not that."

"Then what is it? Are you okay?"

"I'm fine," she said. "It's just...so *sad*."

"What's sad? That Snoopy got cancer? Look at him, he's fine!"

"No." She took a deep breath. "*Everything* is sad."

James cocked his head to the side. "I'm going to need a little more detail on that."

Juliet wiped away the tears on her cheeks, struggling to stop crying. James reached into the backseat and pulled out a handful of napkins. He handed one to Juliet.

"I'm sorry I don't have any tissues," he said. "I save most of my prime-time crying and good tissues for when I'm at home."

The image of James sitting in his multimillion-dollar condo, high in the New York skyline, crying into a wad of hundred dollar bills popped into her head. She let out a laugh.

It seemed so ridiculous; she'd never seen James cry, and she couldn't imagine why he would. At this point especially, his life must be perfect and exactly what he wanted it to be.

Even in high school he had it made. He was a starter on the football team, had a great smile and those sparkling blue eyes – he looked like he could be an Abercrombie and Fitch model.

Juliet was a year younger than him and they never once spoke when they were in high school. They ran in entirely different crowds. The only modeling that Juliet could've done then was for mom jeans in the Sears catalog.

He handed her another tissue. "Yeah, whenever my dad insults me in front of the entire staff, I always laugh. But on the inside, I'm crying, and then I go home and cry in front of the fireplace."

Juliet snorted. "You have a fireplace? Don't you live in a condo?"

"It's electric. Doesn't really do anything."

"But it's good to cry in front of?" Juliet said with a smile.

Maybe his life wasn't entirely perfect. She knew him better than most – or at least, she used to – and it wasn't fair of her to assume that his life was perfect just because he was rich.

His mom died when he was younger, and his dad was less than an ideal parent. Even though his dad was a brilliant scientist who built a successful drug company and was respected by his employees, he was a lackluster father.

James always struggled with trying to please him. Though clearly, his father must be happy with him now. James was a company man for sure.

"Oh, it's the best," he continued. "I cry in front of it, feeling so very sorry for myself, and the flames dry my tears."

"They do not!" laughed Juliet. "You'd have to hold your face up really close."

"I do," he said solemnly. "I dry my tears with fire. Fake fire. I have to make it somewhat manly, you know, because I cry so much."

Juliet blew her nose into one of the napkins. "Of course."

She took a deep breath, trying to steady herself so she could explain why she was crying. James pulled out a McDonald's bag from the back seat for her to toss the tissue into.

"Lots of things make me sad," she finally said. "It makes me sad that Snoopy got cancer. It makes me sad that there are so many kids with special needs who can't afford to go to a therapy like this. It makes me sad that there's so much injustice in the world..." Her voice trailed off.

James waited a moment before responding. "That took quite a leap – from feeling sad for Snoopy and the kids, right into feeling sad about the entire world."

She sighed. How could she explain it to someone like James? Someone who had the world handed to him? He'd always had enough money for everything he ever wanted. He didn't even know what it was like to need something and be unable to get it.

The very fact that he and his father were billionaires in a world where people couldn't afford care for their sick kids – how could she explain that to him? When his dad had dozens of luxury sports cars, and her dad, at age 55, had dentures because he never could afford to go to the dentist growing up?

There was no way he would ever understand. Even if he didn't own a yacht and spend all of his money on gold toilets, or whatever rich people spent their money on, he was still one of them.

"Hey," he said softly. "I know that the world can be a terrible place. And it's unfair, and it's cruel, and bad things happen to good people. But you've always dedicated yourself to trying to make the world better, however you could. That means something."

Juliet's lip started to quiver. Why did he have to go and say things like that? She wanted to answer, but she knew that if she spoke, she would start crying again. Instead, she nodded in agreement.

"That's why I've always been so inspired by you. When things are dark and bleak, you have always been a beam of light."

Oh, now he'd gone too far. "Alright, that's enough for you," she said.

"I mean it! You've always known what you wanted, and you've never let anyone stop you. And what you've wanted was to help others, not to enrich yourself. I wish I could be more like you."

"Uh huh," she said. "We need to get going, there's a snowstorm coming into Cleveland, and we need to meet with a bunch of people tomorrow early in the morning. We can't miss it."

"We won't miss it, don't worry. And you can't just change the subject like that."

"I'm not changing the subject, I'm just stating a fact. We need to move."

"Let me continue talking as I move us in the direction of Cleveland," he said. "If I were more like you, I wouldn't be in the situation that I'm in now."

She scrunched her eyebrows. "What situation? You mean you'd have ten billion dollars instead of five billion?"

He put the car into drive. "How rich do you think I am? I don't have five billion dollars."

She crossed her arms. "Two billion?"

He shook his head. "I don't know. It mostly belongs to the company. I didn't really make it, and my dad will never let me forget it."

"Yet he's still going to make you CEO when he retires. It doesn't seem *that* tragic."

James smiled. "He's trying to do that, but I fail him at every turn."

Juliet laughed. "I highly doubt that."

He shot her a mischievous look. "Oh, you'd be surprised. I've been nothing but a stream of disappointments to him for the last five years."

"He always had high standards," Juliet said with a shrug.

"Yeah, and I never should've tried to meet them in the first place. I never should've set foot in New York. I just should have done what I wanted to do with my life."

Wow. She'd never heard James talk like this. When they were both in college, his thoughts on success were very different. There was no reasoning with him – it was almost as though his sanity depended on convincing his dad that he had some worth and could run the company.

As much as her own parents yelled and carried on, they always were proud of everything that she and her brother did. James never once had his father's approval, and he never stopped chasing it.

"I thought you were doing what you wanted? You wanted to be a successful businessman. And I'd say you're pretty successful."

"I wanted to be a zookeeper like Steve Irwin, and you know it," he said without looking away from the road. "My dad always thought that was some kind of a silly childhood dream, though. I believed him, so I decided that it was, too."

"And it wasn't?"

"It's one of the only two things that I can't stop thinking about. I use every business trip to go to a new zoo. I've been to 36 different zoos in the United States, and four zoos in Europe. More and more I find myself daydreaming during meetings about being outside in a pair of khaki shorts." James laughed, shaking his head. "I know it sounds wacky. But I can't tell anyone this, they'll think I'm crazy and the stock price of the company will probably plummet."

"Well if you randomly told them that you wanted to wrestle crocodiles, they might think you're crazy. And they might be right."

"Crikey, isn't she a beauty?" James replied in his best Australian accent.

"Still working on that accent, huh?"

He sighed. "I mean what I said. Seeing you after all these years, still doing the right thing, still doing what you think is important. I just feel like I wasted the last five years of my life."

This was getting a little too heavy. Juliet didn't need to play James' therapist, or hear him say any more nice things about her. She had a fleeting feeling that he might be trying to manipulate her – but no, it seemed too genuine. She had no idea where it was all coming from.

"I don't know what to tell you, James. If you don't like your life, change it."

"It's not that simple."

She flipped on the radio. "It *is* that simple. It's just not easy."

They rode along in silence for a few minutes. James seemed lost in thought. Juliet took the opportunity to check the weather for their upcoming drive. It was a long drive, and a snowstorm was supposed to hit the Cleveland area pretty hard during the last two hours of their drive.

"Maybe we should stop early and wait out the storm," said Juliet.

James made a face. "Nah, we'll be fine."

Four hours into their drive, things were definitely not fine. Almost four inches of snow accumulated in a matter of hours and the highway was completely white. Most drivers were staying in the right lane, driving slowly with their flashers on.

Not James. He insisted on staying in the left lane, passing the rest of the cars.

"They're going so slow that they're actually being hazards. You can't drive that slow in the snow," he reasoned. "You can get stuck."

"They're going at least 20 or 30 miles an hour. That's plenty of speed to not get stuck," Juliet snapped. "It's getting worse by the minute. Let's just pull over and find somewhere to wait out the night."

"Trust me, this car can handle the snow."

"I'm not someone who cowers at an inch of snow," she said, her voice rising. "But I'm telling you, road conditions are only going to get worse. We don't need to get to Cleveland tonight, we can get there in the morning after they've had some time to clear the roads."

"I'm going to get you there on time," he replied.

"This is ridiculous." She firmly crossed her arms on her chest. She held them so tightly that there were deep red marks on her skin.

"Watch out," she said, "this truck on the right is being really aggressive."

Almost as though on cue, the black pickup truck cut in front of them. The back end of the truck drifted too far and the driver tried to correct it – first right, then left, then right again. Each swing of the vehicle was more extreme than the last, and finally, the driver lost control completely, spinning sideways and blocking both lanes.

"Not good, not good," yelled James. There were three more cars ahead of them now also trapped in the mess; James quickly turned the steering wheel to the left.

At first, he was successful in avoiding the other cars and the bits of broken-off plastic bumpers. The Porsche did well, tearing through a snowy embankment, until another car smashed into it from behind, causing a tailspin.

Juliet heard herself screaming, but in a moment, their car was stopped, pushed off to the side, with the front of the car nestled into a pile of snow.

"Are you okay?" asked James.

The seatbelt had held her firmly in place, and though startled, Juliet didn't feel pain anywhere.

"Yeah, I think I am. Are you?"

"Yeah, I'm fine." He peered out of the window, straining his neck. "It looks like there are at least ten cars that slid off the road."

Juliet rubbed her face in her hands. If he'd listened to her, they could've avoided this entire situation. What if someone was really hurt back there?

It seemed that at least for now, all of the cars were stopped along the highway and no one else could blast through and hit them. She pulled out her phone, dialed 911, and got out of the car without saying another word to James.

Chapter 12

This was bad. This was very bad.

James looked out of the window and saw Juliet popping her head into the car behind them.

He groaned and rubbed his face. Just when things were starting to go well, he blew it. Somehow the airbags didn't deploy – they must not have been hit that hard. Just hard enough to lose control.

It didn't look like anyone's car was terribly damaged, but there were several cars forced off of the road. Maybe they'd all hit an icy patch?

Of course he didn't expect all of that to happen. Of course it would be when Juliet was finally talking to him – he even got her to stop crying.

They were supposed to meet the next group of pets early in the morning, so James wanted to be sure that he got to the hotel with plenty of time. He really thought that he was doing a *good* thing for their cause. Clearly he was wrong.

He got out of the car and caught up to Juliet. "Hey – is everyone okay?"

She responded by pulling up the hood of her jacket and walking away. Clearly she didn't want to talk. James still walked with her from car to car.

Two police officers arrived on the scene fairly quickly. Juliet spoke to one of them, letting them know that so far, she hadn't seen anyone seriously injured.

The second officer came up to James and said, with a laugh, "Look at that fancy Porsche all banged up."

"Yeah, it's a shame," said James. He wasn't going to admit to owning it while the officer was making fun of the damage.

A third police officer joined them. "That car was reported stolen. Just ran the plates."

Huh. Now James *really* didn't plan on telling him that the Porsche was his. Clearly his dad was still salty about the lost investor, but reporting the car stolen was taking it too far.

"Well," said the officer, "the storm isn't supposed to let up for another four hours or so. We can drive all of you to a nearby hotel and you can reassess your cars in the morning."

"That would be wonderful," said James. He spotted Juliet, who was making a beeline for the Porsche. He almost fell over running towards her.

"Juliet, I need a word with you please," he said.

She ignored him, as usual. He had no choice but to step in front of her.

"Listen, we have a bit of a complication. Apparently my dad reported the Porsche as stolen."

She stopped dead in her tracks. "What!"

"You have to keep your voice down. And we can't get anything from the car, this other officer said that he would give us a ride to a hotel. We can come back in the morning for everything once I sort things out with my dad."

She crossed her arms. "We can't leave the camera in the car overnight, it'll be cold and might break."

"No it won't," said James. Truth be told, he had no idea if that was true.

"And what if it does? And we lose all of the footage? Or they put it into evidence and lock it away forever?"

James groaned. "But if we go back to the car they'll see –"

"I don't care! I'm getting the camera!"

She brushed past him; he reached out and grabbed her elbow. "Okay, listen, I need you to distract them. Then I'll go and grab our stuff."

"No! That's ridiculous. Just call your dad and get it straightened out."

"That won't work, because he will tell them to arrest me. I really don't want to spend the night in the county jail."

"Maybe it would do you some good."

"It might," he said, lowering his voice, "but you'll be charged as an accessory to grand theft auto."

"Are you kidding me?" she asked in a hoarse whisper.

"Unfortunately, I'm not."

Juliet gritted her teeth. Clearly, as much as she wanted to yell at him, she wanted to not be arrested more.

James leaned in. "I'll be fast. Just walk like twenty feet away and fall over or something. They'll all come running over."

"That's not going to work," she hissed. "Why would they come over if I fell?"

"Because you're a pretty woman, and it's their duty to protect and serve. But also, and I can't stress this enough, you're a pretty woman."

She turned around to look at the two remaining police officers – the other two were driving people to the hotel. She took a deep breath. "I can't believe this. But fine, I'll do it."

"Thank you," he said.

James made his way towards the Porsche as casually as he could. He kept an eye on Juliet, who walked past the officers, and then one, two, three cars away. Suddenly she slipped and let out a yelp.

Both of the officers looked up immediately.

Bingo.

They didn't hesitate to rush toward her. James dropped to the ground and army crawled through the snow to the far side of the Porsche. He quietly opened the passenger door, reaching in only far enough to grab Juliet's bag, her purse, and the camera bag. Unfortunately, his bag of clothes was in the trunk. He wasn't going to risk getting caught for that.

He closed the door and peeked around the back of the car. The officers were facing away from him, so he stood up quickly and ran towards them.

"My darling, are you okay?" he said.

For the briefest moment, he saw the flash of anger in Juliet's eyes. "Yes, I'm fine, thank you."

Even though she was annoyed, she had to be nice to him. James couldn't help it – he was going to enjoy this opportunity for the brief amount of time that he had it. He put an arm around her.

"I think my wife needs to get somewhere warm. Maybe we can take the next trip over to the hotel?"

"Of course," said the officer. "I think Officer Gear will be back any minute."

"That's perfect," said James, pulling Juliet in tightly.

As soon as the officers turned their backs, Juliet elbowed him in the ribs. He let out a puff of air.

That hurt, but it was still worth it.

Officer Gear arrived and was happy to drive them to a nearby La Quinta. Unfortunately for James, Juliet would not speak to him. Not when they got to the hotel, not when they booked their rooms, and not when he said goodnight after walking her to her door.

He knew that they were supposed to meet a group of dogs and their owners the next morning – he thought it was at 9 o'clock. That was going to be tough, because they couldn't take his car. Well – they could try, but they might be arrested.

That wasn't ideal, so he decided to call in a favor from one of his friends from work. The salesman had a coordinator on staff – Rachel. She helped them book flights, keep their calendars, and not mess up their schedules. He gave Rachel a call, and luckily she answered.

"Hey – I need a big favor. Can you get me a car in a snowstorm?"

"Of course," she said casually. "Where are you?"

The next morning, James sent Juliet a text message at 6:30.

No response.

At seven he knocked on her door. She didn't answer, but he could hear her moving around.

"Come on, I can hear you in there," he said through the door.

Still no response.

"I fixed our car problem."

The door flung open. "Oh yeah? Does it involve either of us having to post bail?"

"No."

"I'm finding my own car, thank you," she said. She closed the door in his face.

James stood there for a moment. He knew he deserved it, but she had to give him some credit.

"You won't be able to rent a car before we need to be there. I have a car waiting in the parking lot."

The door whipped open again. "Great. Give me the keys."

"No, because you'll leave me behind and I'll be stranded."

"Why don't you go and reclaim your car from the police?" she said.

"Because I've still got work to do before I get arrested for the week!"

She scoffed. "You mean more cars to crash?"

"I am really sorry about that. I was driving perfectly safely until that truck lost control ahead of us."

She nodded slowly. "Oh, right. It's almost like I told you to go slower and get out of the left lane, but you didn't, and we ended up in a crash."

"But I didn't cause us to – "

She cut him off. "Not your fault, right James?"

He frowned. "That's not fair, you know that wasn't my fault."

"Don't you know that you're supposed to drive expecting other people to do stupid things?"

"I do now!" he said, raising his voice.

She stuck out her hand. "I don't believe you. Let me drive."

"Only if you promise to take me with you."

She rolled her eyes. "Fine, you can come. It's the last stop anyways."

"It is?" His heart fell. "Are you sure you don't want to find some more people to talk to?"

"The video has to be submitted in two days and I'm lucky that Greg even agreed to edit this on such short notice."

He didn't expect their trip to end so abruptly. Or so badly.

"Okay, you can drive. Let's go."

Juliet didn't budge. "Where're the keys?"

"I don't have them yet."

"Do you even have a car?"

"Yes." He paused. "I think so."

She sighed, clearly weighing her options. "Let me make sure I have everything in my bag."

Before he could answer, she closed the door on him again.

They checked out of the hotel and made their way to the parking lot. They were met by a man in a suit and white gloves. James cringed – Juliet wouldn't appreciate the formality of it all. He handed James the keys to a Jaguar.

"Thank you," James said before turning over the keys to Juliet. "I was told that this was the best winter driver they had available."

Juliet nodded and made her way to the driver's seat. James quickly rushed to the passenger seat to make sure that she didn't drive off without him.

"Well," she said once inside, "it's a good thing you're letting me drive."

"Why?"

"Because this car is a stick shift. I guess you forgot to tell them that you can't drive stick."

"That detail did slip my mind," he said with a smile.

She didn't smile back before starting the engine.

They made it to the meeting place only 10 minutes late, which James didn't think was too bad considering everything that happened, but Juliet felt terrible about making the dog owners wait.

This time, they met with a group of seven people whose dogs all had osteosarcoma. Since Juliet was no longer speaking to him, James had all morning to get to know everyone in the group. Each of the dogs had bone cancer in one of their legs and underwent an amputation and chemotherapy before getting Delicaid.

"We know from humans that bone cancer is one of the most painful cancers," one of the owners, Sandy, explained to James. "Without the amputation, my Bella would've been unable to walk. In no time, the aggressive tumor would've destroyed so much of the bone in her back leg that it would've snapped it in half. And we would've had to put her down."

"That's awful," said James. He watched as Bella, a three-legged German Shepherd, ducked and hopped, wrestling with another dog.

Sandy continued. "Even with the amputation and the chemo, the cancer is so aggressive that most dogs may not even make it a year. With the Delicaid, Bella has lived *three years* past her diagnosis."

"That's incredible!" said James.

Sandy smiled. "It's been such a blessing. Such a blessing."

They spent a total of four hours getting videos of the dogs and their owners. James couldn't believe how full of life these three-legged dogs were. They ran, they jumped, they played. Some of them moved so fast that he couldn't tell that they only had three legs until they stopped. It was amazing.

They got back to the car and Juliet decided to speak to him again. "I bought a bus ticket. I'm going back to Lansing tonight. I'd appreciate it if you could give me a ride to the station."

"Of course, I'd be happy to. Are you sure that you don't want to _ "

"No. Just the bus station."

He couldn't argue with her. He didn't know what to say after messing up so badly. Obviously any points he'd won up to now were lost. "Do you mind driving again?"

They drove in silence for twenty minutes. When they got to the station, she got out of the car, thanked him for his help, and walked through the front doors without looking back.

Chapter 13

Juliet took a seat in the lobby and pulled out her laptop. She had enough time before her bus arrived to connect to the internet and send the remaining videos to Greg.

There were a few problems that slowed her down, but she didn't mind. Not only did it help fill the time she was waiting for the bus, it also took up all of her mental space.

Juliet typed out an email thanking Greg for editing the video together and then got on the bus for the seven hour ride. It wasn't something she was looking forward to. She had a book in her bag, but it was a romance and she wasn't in the mood for that.

She settled into her seat and thought that maybe she could take a nap for a few hours. This hope was quickly dashed when two college aged girls settled in behind her, chatting loudly and excitedly.

Juliet took a deep breath and closed her eyes anyway. Immediately, the image of the car spinning out of control flashed in her mind.

She opened her eyes and touched the spot on her shoulder where the seatbelt left a bruise. Maybe she should see her doctor when she got home? But she didn't have time for that. She needed to get back to work.

Juliet pulled out her phone and decided to look at the news. Surprisingly, there wasn't a story about their ten car pileup on the highway. It must be a common enough occurrence that no one cared.

A morbid curiosity got the better of her and she googled James' name to see if there was a story on the news about him being arrested for stealing a car.

He was such a ridiculous human being. Not only did he almost kill her by driving like a maniac in the snow, he almost got her arrested! She couldn't decide which was worse.

Clearly he didn't realize how serious this all was. If she got arrested for a *felony*, she could've lost her veterinarian's license. Also, someone could've been really hurt in that crash. Or the camera could have been destroyed!

What did he care? He had all the money in the world. He could buy himself a new camera or a new Porsche or a judge to get him out of jail.

Juliet let out a huff and shifted uncomfortably in her seat. She told herself that she wasn't going to obsess over James the whole way home. Yet she couldn't think about anything else – why was that?

It wasn't because she liked him. Definitely not that. They had fun on this trip, sure. A lot more fun than she expected to have. But he still ruined everything in the end because of his stubbornness and inability to accept fault.

She should have seen that coming. Maybe that's what bothered her so much – she should've known better because she *knew* what James was like.

They dated for three years, and she'd been let down by him before. Why did she think this time would be any different?

Yeah, that was it. She was angry at herself for trusting him again. Even if it was just trusting him to drive her around safely, it was too much. He couldn't even handle that responsibility. While she was angry at him, she was more so angry at herself. It felt like...well, it felt like the last year of the relationship all over again.

Their relationship started out like a cheesy romantic comedy. Initially, James sought out Juliet as his tutor. She couldn't believe that she was going to tutor *the* James Balin in biology.

They'd never spoken in high school, so she was a bit afraid that he would be a jerk, but she took the job because she badly needed the money. Plus, at the very least, it'd be a good story to tell her friends. And when James turned out to be charming, and funny, and sweet... it made for more than a good story for her friends.

He was an avid animal lover, like she was, and he was enthralled by her plans to go to veterinary school. He asked her all kinds of questions about the process and what the classes would be like.

It wasn't that he wanted to try to get into veterinary school, too – he admitted that he didn't stand a chance because he was terrible at science. Despite this, he was a biology minor. It was one of the many things he did to try to impress his dad.

Nothing worked, of course, and James struggled to pass the classes. Luckily Juliet was a great tutor. She was so great that after one semester, James didn't really need her anymore. She'd taught him *how* to study biology – her method was to make him explain the notes out loud with minimal peeking at the material. It was a trick she picked up in high school that ensured she fully understood what she was talking about.

She couldn't help but develop a bit of a crush on him during tutoring, but never in a million years did she imagine that he would feel even remotely the same. So when she received a text message asking if she'd like to go to dinner, she was shocked.

At first, she assumed that he must need help with biology lab or something. She didn't even tell her friends because she didn't want them to tease her and say that he liked her when she knew that couldn't possibly be true.

Yet he *did* like her. He told her that evening that he couldn't stop thinking about her and missed spending time with her. All the while, Juliet felt like her head was spinning. She loved spending time with him too, but she never planned to say those words out loud.

The first six months of their relationship felt like a dream. James was an exceedingly thoughtful and attentive boyfriend. They had so much fun together, too. Things were perfect until he graduated and headed to New York City.

The bus pulled into a rest stop and Juliet was jarred from her thoughts. She didn't realize they were already three hours into their journey. She decided to get out, stretch her legs, and maybe get a snack.

After stopping in the bathroom, she wandered into the gift shop to see what looked good. She paused in front of a huge display of Pringles.

Of course there would be a seven foot tall display of Pringles. They were James' favorite.

She picked up a can of the sour cream and onion and allowed herself to feel a bit nostalgic. The last time that she had Pringles was on a bus ride a lot like this. She took a bus from Ann Arbor to New York City to visit James. He offered to buy her plane tickets, but she felt weird accepting something so expensive from him.

He'd always say, "What's money worth anyways if you can't spend it on someone you love?"

She never knew how to respond to that, so she'd just tell him she was sticking with the bus.

Juliet remembered feeling tense for most of the ride. It was long – fifteen hours – but she'd hoped to sleep for most of it since it was overnight.

She had little luck with that, though. She felt nervous about seeing James. Everything about the relationship changed when he moved to New York.

He spent most of his time working and they didn't talk nearly as much as they did before. He made new friends that Juliet always felt uncomfortable around. Half of them were as career driven as he was, uninterested in talking about anything unless it related to making more money. The other half were these stunning woman who were convinced they were going to make it big as models.

Juliet never fully expressed how these people made her feel, because she couldn't put her finger on it. It wasn't until years later that she processed what bothered her so much.

The beautiful women made Juliet feel insecure – not because she was jealous, exactly, but because they were so sure of themselves and men always paid attention to them. Juliet never knew how to dress when she went out with them, though one would always make a patronizing comment like, "I love how you just go with casual."

The rest of his friends couldn't speak to her without making it obvious that it was a chore. Or that it was like talking to a little sibling, and they were only polite as long as they had to be before moving onto something more interesting.

They made it clear that she wasn't one of them, and they did it with a smile.

Juliet picked up a can of sour cream and onion Pringles on her way to NYC on that last trip. She thought it would be sweet, especially because James said that he couldn't find them in any stores around his apartment. It wasn't the most exciting gift, but she figured it'd be the last time she'd make this particular bus trip – she'd gotten into veterinary school in Austin and James promised to transfer to the Austin branch of Balin Labs as soon as he could.

When he picked her up from the bus station, he surprised her with the news that he was having "a small get together" to celebrate his promotion at work. As other partygoers brought fancy champagne or artwork as gifts, Juliet showed up with that can of Pringles, like an idiot.

She had nothing appropriate to wear and as always, felt underdressed and awkward. James was busy welcoming people and making sure that the party was running smoothly. Juliet was pushed off in the corner of the kitchen, telling people where the ice bucket was. One of James' friends from work, Logan, took a shift making polite conversation with her.

"It's amazing that James has been promoted so quickly," he commented.

Juliet smiled. "He is amazing. And it doesn't hurt that his dad is the head of the company."

"Oh – I wasn't implying – "

"No," Juliet said quickly, "I didn't mean that. We joke because his dad is so tough."

"Right, right," Logan replied. "He can probably afford to actually move to Manhattan now, though."

Juliet laughed. "Well I'm sure that money will go a lot further in Austin."

"Austin?" Logan turned to face her. She finally had his interest. "It's going to be hard for him to be the lead salesman of the North Eastern territory from Texas."

Of course. This party was supposed to celebrate his promotion – the one that kept him from keeping his promise to her.

"Oh," she touched her forehead, trying to hide her reddening cheeks. "Right. What was I thinking?"

Logan gave her a stiff smile and excused himself.

The next hour of the party was a blur. James eventually came over to explain to Juliet how important the promotion was, and how moving to Austin now would jeopardize his career, and she would understand in the end, right?

She didn't want to cry in public, so she refused to talk to him about it then. She was only able to tell him that she was shocked and disappointed.

He got a glint in his eye. "Well, before you get upset –"

He grabbed a glass, clinking a spoon on the side.

"Everyone," he called out. "Can I have your attention for a moment?"

The room settled down.

"As excited as I am to be taking the next step with Balin, it doesn't compare to how excited I feel to be with this beautiful woman. Juliet, you are the most wonderful person that I've ever met. I can't imagine my life without you. Will you do me the honor of being my wife?"

He got down on one knee and pulled a ring box from his pocket. The women around them gasped – it was a *huge* stone. Ridiculous, even.

Juliet looked at him in horror. How could he do something as stupid as proposing to her in front of all these people? Though she was able to stave off the tears when she heard that he wouldn't be moving as he'd promised, this was too much. Her vision started to blur – she ran from the room and out of his life forever.

Juliet set the can of Pringles back on the shelf. She was more of a Combos girl anyway.

Chapter 14

For an hour, James sat in the parking lot of the bus station. His reasoning was twofold – first, he wanted to make sure that Juliet's bus came and she wouldn't end up stranded. Second, he couldn't drive stick shift, so he was stuck with the car until the company came to pick up both him and it. He finally decided to press the pickup request button on the dashboard.

Since he abandoned his bag in the Porsche, he wasn't able to charge his phone and the battery was dead. It gave him an excuse not to call his dad for just a bit longer – he knew he'd get an earful about leaving the Porsche in the snow.

Without his phone to distract him, James sat there daydreaming and staring at the front doors to the bus station. People filed in and out, but Juliet remained inside.

When Neal, the driver, came to pick him up, James asked him to wait for just a minute as he checked the bus station lobby. It was possible that the snow might've canceled some of the bus routes and Juliet would be stranded in Cleveland.

Fortunately – or, unfortunately for James – Juliet was nowhere to be seen. Though he was glad that she was able to catch a bus, he was disappointed that he wouldn't get to see her again.

Despite this hiccup, he was determined to get back in her good graces. He didn't care if he had to quit his job at Balin Labs in order to show her that he was serious – all he cared about was winning her back.

Neal drove him to the main office and James was able to set aside his phone to charge. Since Neal still had two hours on the clock, James decided to treat him to dinner at the nearest restaurant that was still open – Red Lobster.

Despite being complete strangers, they had a lovely time. James learned that Neal started out as a used car salesman, eventually moving up to luxury car sales, and finally to this high-end business of catering to the whims of annoyingly rich people.

"I've got to say," said Neal with a mouthful of biscuit, "you're one of my favorite clients by far. You barely drove the car, you didn't yell at my staff, and then you took me out for a romantic evening."

James almost choked on his water. "You've been a lovely date."

When they returned to the headquarters, James turned on his phone and was surprised to see that he had several missed calls from his dad. There was even a voicemail. Puzzled, James dialed in to listen to it.

"James," it started out, "it's Richard."

He let out a sigh. Why couldn't he ever get a message that said something simple like 'Hey, it's Dad, how are you?'

"My assistant tells me that the Porsche was involved in a multi-car pileup outside of Cleveland. Please, uh, give me a call as soon as you get this."

Now that was something. His dad must've gotten a call from the police that his "stolen" car was discovered abandoned and damaged in the snow. Was James fooling himself, or did his dad sound concerned? That seemed about as close as his dad ever got to concerned. Or at least as close as he would show.

James had the petty thought of purposely not calling his dad back, just to make him sweat. That would show him! But he quickly dismissed it, knowing that it was cruel and wouldn't achieve anything.

He dialed his dad's cell phone number.

"Hello, Richard Balin speaking."

Again with the formalities. He clearly saw James' name pop up on the caller ID. Whatever.

"Hey Dad, it's me."

Richard cleared his throat. "Hold on a second, let me step out of this meeting."

James waited almost a full minute as his dad gave a few last instructions before leaving whatever meeting he was in.

Finally, he said, "Okay, what's up?"

Oh, so now that he knew that James wasn't killed in a snowy crash, he was going to play cool?

James could play cool too. "I don't know. I got your voicemail that you wanted me to call you."

"Right. Yeah. I got a call about the Porsche."

"The stolen one, you mean?" asked James, unable to keep the edge out of his voice.

There was a pause before his dad responded. "You left me no choice, taking off like that without a word."

"Come on, Dad. You basically ran me out of the city, what was I supposed to do? Stay there and beg for your forgiveness?"

"You ran off to Cleveland, of all places."

"Alright, well I don't know if you were worried, but if you were, I'm okay. I'm going to leave the Porsche where it is so I don't get arrested, which would cause problems for your company's reputation."

"You don't have to worry about that," his dad responded in an even tone. "I told them that it wasn't stolen, just that I didn't know you'd borrowed it. It's being repaired as we speak."

James sighed. "Okay. Do you want me to drive it back, or are you having it shipped?"

"That's fine, you can drive it. Take your time."

"Thanks." He waited – maybe his dad would say something nice?

James finally broke the silence, "Alright, well, have a good night."

"You too."

He ended the call and resisted the urge to throw his phone across the room. No wonder Juliet wanted nothing to do with him. The man on the other end of that call was supposed to be his role model, the one who was supposed to show him how to love and how to live his life well. No wonder James was such a disappointment.

It didn't matter. That was in the past. James wasn't going to let his dad define his life anymore – he'd allowed that to go on for too long. And what did he have to show for it?

Nothing. Absolutely nothing.

He had a job where he'd clawed his way to the top by working crazy hours and traveling most of the year. His employees did the same, driven by their own misguided illusions as to what was important in life.

He drove fancy cars and lived in a fancy condo, sure, but he'd never actually *wanted* any of that. It brought him no joy. It was all just necessary to fuel the image of a successful businessman, training to take over a company that he didn't care about.

Yet somehow, his dream of being a zookeeper is what his dad thought was crazy.

"You're going to shovel animal dung all day?" he'd say. "And you think that'll make you happy?"

But James thought that *this* life was crazy. What was the point of it, any of it, if he wasn't happy? Maybe his dad needed to work all the time to fill the void that appeared after his mother's death. But James didn't; though he missed her, it wasn't a reason to waste the rest of his life.

He took a deep breath and set the phone call out of his mind. None of that mattered. He could take or leave the job. He didn't care about it right now. All he cared about was apologizing to Juliet and showing to her – proving to her – that he was different than before.

James set his mind to his next task: ensuring that Juliet won the funding for her clinic. He made a call to his assistant Logan.

He answered right away. "Hey boss, what's up?"

"Hey Logan, do you have a minute?"

"Sure."

"Did you get the information for that drug?"

"Yup," he replied. "I sent you some stuff to your email. The company that makes Delicaid is InnoCangen."

James laughed. "What a name."

"I know, doesn't really roll off the tongue. But as it turns out, we *do* have a contact there."

"Awesome! Who is it?"

"Kylie Simpson. Do you remember her?"

James frowned. "Not really."

"She interned here. Not in our department, but she was a member of the marketing team. I think she had a thing for you."

James felt his ears growing hot. "Was she the one who kept bringing danishes to my office?"

"Yeah! That was her."

Well, that made it awkward. "I don't want her to think I decided to return the crush after all these years. Can I have a meeting with her that legitimately looks professional?"

Logan laughed. "Of course. If you're sure that's what you want? She was pretty cute, I don't know why you – "

"Thanks Logan, but I'm sure."

"Alright, fine. Then the only thing you can do is meet with her and try to recruit her back."

James groaned. "Can't I say that I'm looking into...I don't know, using their drug for my cat?"

"No," Logan responded flatly. "We have a really similar drug that's a bit ahead in clinical trials than theirs is. If they're smart, they'll be our competition soon."

"Ugh, fine. Could we use her on staff?"

Logan scoffed. "I don't know, you're the boss!"

"Whatever, I'll figure it out. We can always use good people." He paused. "Was she good?"

"She brought in all those danishes, that has to count for something."

James rubbed his forehead. "Alright, well, can you set up a meeting for me with her? Tomorrow? And get me a plane out there."

"You got it."

"Thanks Logan."

James took a deep breath. He needed to make sure not to lead this girl on. Maybe she had a husband by now, who knew. It didn't matter.

He needed to casually feel out the criteria for the winner of the funding. And make sure that Kylie knew that Juliet's video and program was the most deserving.

Should be a piece of cake.

Chapter 15

The bus ride was uneventful and Juliet got back to her apartment early in the morning. She didn't manage to sleep much, so after washing her face and brushing her teeth, she crawled into bed to catch an hour of sleep before going to work. Luckily, her dad fixed his car, so she borrowed her mom's car. She was no longer dependent on James.

The clinic schedule was quite full that day – they needed to catch up after Juliet was off. She was glad to be back; she didn't want her thoughts to linger on what happened over the past few days.

Oddly, James didn't try to contact her at all. At first she was relieved, but then she felt a bit disappointed, and then angry at herself for feeling disappointed. Maybe she could've been nicer to him. After all, he was a huge help, even if he was a bit of an idiot. And a bad driver.

Why *was* James so willing to help, though? Juliet still couldn't put her finger on it. He probably thought that she had some special knowledge about the drug, and after he realized that she didn't, he disappeared back to his fabulous life.

She told herself to stop being silly and focus on work. The day went by quickly and when she got home, she made a sandwich for dinner and went straight to bed.

The rest of the week carried on in the same way. Greg sent her the final versions of the videos – they both made her cry, and she watched them at least ten times each. She submitted them and tried not to obsess.

Juliet managed to catch up on sleep and was back to feeling normal by Saturday clinic. Well – mostly normal. She managed to forget one important thing.

"Are you excited for our double date tonight?" asked Sophie, one of the veterinary technicians.

Juliet groaned. "I completely forgot about that."

"Don't make that face!" Sophie slapped her on the shoulder. "It's going to be fun!"

Juliet was looking forward to spending the evening alone, in front of her TV, in sweatpants. How could she have agreed to something like this? Sophie must've really talked it up.

Also, it was always easier to agree to things when they were far away. She could imagine herself feeling sociable and full of energy when something like a double date was a month in the future. When it was a few hours away, it seemed like a nightmare.

"What's this guy's name again?" asked Juliet.

"James."

Juliet felt her stomach drop. "James?"

"But," Sophie continued, "he goes by Jim. He works with Leo. I've met him a few times, and he's a *really* nice guy."

A really nice guy. If Juliet had a dollar for every time someone tried to force *a really nice guy* on her and he ended up being a weirdo, a jerk, or a bore, she'd have at *least* $15.

Though it wasn't a ton of money, it was a ton of bad dates.

Juliet sighed. There was no getting out of it now. "Where are we going again?"

"The Spicy Pepper."

Oh. That was a good restaurant; at least Juliet could get some tacos out of it, and they always served hot tortilla chips there, too.

"Okay, it's a date."

Sophie beamed. "See you at seven!"

Clinic ran late and at the end of the day, one of their regulars called in a panic. Their dog ate an entire plate of chicken wings, bones included.

Juliet didn't mind staying after closing and told them to bring him in right away. She induced vomiting and within moments, a pile of mostly intact chicken wings appeared on the clinic floor.

After rushing home, she took a shower and tried to get dressed for her date. She wasn't sure what to wear; she never wore makeup, unless she was going to a wedding or something, so that was out. Most of her wardrobe consisted of clothes that were comfortable to go hiking in, but not necessarily nice enough to go to dinner in. Even her jeans looked worn out.

She stood in front of her dresser with her arms crossed. She didn't want to try too hard, either, and make this guy think that she was desperate or something, because that definitely wasn't the case.

Embarrassingly, the newest thing she had in her closet was a sweater that her mom bought her because it was on sale and "It was *just* the right color!"

Juliet slipped into it and studied herself in the mirror. It was a nice sweater, and somehow the light blue seemed to make her skin look nice, even though she hadn't seen the sun in months. She decided that no one needed to know that her mom bought it for her and she headed out the door.

When Juliet got to the restaurant, she sent a text to Sophie to see if they'd arrived yet. She didn't want to go inside and end up alone with this guy.

Instead of going in, she sat in her dark car, feeling like a creep, watching each person that came in or out.

Sophie clearly missed her text, because Juliet watched as she and her husband rushed into the restaurant. Juliet took a deep breath and closed her eyes. She reminded herself that she agreed to this, and it would be impossibly rude to back out now. Plus, she was hungry and it was getting cold in the car.

It wasn't hard to find Sophie and her husband Leo inside, especially because Sophie was waving and yelling, "Juliet! Over here!"

Oh boy. This was already worse than she imagined.

"Hey guys, good to see you," she said, taking a seat across from Sophie.

"Hey Juliet," said Leo.

Sophie shushed him. "He should be here any minute."

Juliet forced a smile. "Great."

She opened up the menu, surveying the appetizers closely because she didn't think she could make it much longer without food.

"What do you guys think? Chips and salsa? Or should we go for the gold and get chips and guacamole?"

Leo opened his mouth to respond but Sophie beat him to it. "Whatever, you pick. Hey Jim!"

Juliet turned away from the menu to look up at the man approaching the table. He offered an awkward wave.

For some reason, Sophie stood up. "Jim, I'd like you to meet my friend Juliet McCarron."

He shot his hand across the table, almost knocking over Juliet's glass of water. "Nice to meet you."

She moved the glass out of the way and shook his hand. "Nice to meet you, too."

He took a seat. Juliet knew that she should try to make conversation with him, but what she really wanted to do was put an order in for an appetizer. She caught sight of a waitress walking by and made eye contact.

"You folks ready to order?" the waitress said, pulling out a notepad.

"I would love to put in an order for some chips and guacamole," said Juliet. "If that's okay with everyone?"

She looked around the table and everyone nodded.

"Alright, they'll be right out," said the waitress.

Juliet looked at the menu one more time and decided that she needed to make a decision so she wasn't staring at the menu forever. She decided to go with the fish tacos.

"So, James who goes by Jim, what brings you to Lansing?" Juliet asked.

He set his menu down. "Oh, you know, work."

"Oh," she said. "Do you have any family in the area?"

"No," he responded before looking back at the menu.

Oh boy. A real talker. She wasn't in the mood to think of questions so that he could respond with one-word answers. She had nothing against shy people – she often felt quite shy herself. But if this guy wasn't even going to try, then she wasn't going to either.

Sophie stepped in. "Jim moved here from Florida. The company recruited him."

"Oh, that's neat. Do you miss Florida?"

"Yeah," he said without looking up from the menu. "It's way too cold here."

"Oh come on," Leo said. "You haven't given any winter sports a chance yet. Let me take you out on my snowmobile."

Jim laughed. "No thank you. I've managed to stay inside all winter without getting hurt and I'm not going to risk it now."

Juliet couldn't help herself. "Not one for adventure, eh?"

"Oh, I love adventure. Just not in the snow. I actually worked it out with the boss so I can work from home on snowy days."

That seemed like a very Floridian thing to do. In contrast, Juliet and everyone she knew tried to one up each other every winter in driving in worse and worse snowy conditions.

"Sometimes it's fun to drive in the snow," she said.

"Oh, yeah, I agree. It is really fun," said Jim with a bright smile.

That seemed like an odd thing to say for someone who *just* admitted to being afraid of the snow, but Juliet didn't have a chance to address it; the waitress came back to take their orders.

Juliet ordered fish tacos, Leo ordered carnitas tacos, and Sophie ordered a chicken tostada. Jim asked to go last. Juliet was curious as to what he was going to pick.

"I'd like to get the Everything Burrito, but please hold the bean sprouts. And can you make sure that the black beans on there are really watery?"

The waitress frowned. "What do you mean watery? If it's watery, your burrito will fall apart."

"Trust me, I always get burritos this way. I like the bean juice."

Bean juice.

The waitress' face remained expressionless as she wrote down his order, but Juliet was dying inside. She knew that the waitress was going to go back and tell everyone what a weirdo this guy was.

"Okay, anything else?"

"One more thing," said Jim. "I'm allergic to avocado, so can you please make sure there's no avocado on my meal?"

"Of course."

Oh dear. Allergic to avocado and Juliet just ordered a bunch of guacamole for the table?

"I am so sorry for ordering guacamole," said Juliet. "I had no idea that you were allergic to it."

He laughed. "Oh, it's no big deal. I just won't have any of it. You can't really avoid it at a Mexican restaurant."

"Right," Juliet said weakly. Why didn't he just say something? Now she felt like a jerk.

"So Juliet's been away for a few days trying to win a fundraiser for our clinic," said Sophie with a coy smile.

"Wow, that's *so* interesting." Jim leaned in.

He was too close to her face; Juliet sat back. "Thanks. We'll see if we get the funding."

"I just think that it's *so* interesting that you're a veterinarian," Jim continued.

"Oh. Why?"

"It's just – uncommon." He cleared his throat. "What made you want to be a vet?"

"You know, the usual. I love animals. Wanted to save every one of them and help them live forever."

"Plus you're really smart," added Sophie.

Jim smiled broadly. "I always knew that I wanted to be a programmer. My parents got me my first computer when I was five. They were amazed by how good I was at using it, and by the time I was ten, I was a real whiz kid."

A whiz kid? Who says that about themselves?

"Really?" Juliet said. She had to force herself not to yawn. "That's cool."

Jim nodded. "In high school I was the lead for the design tech team. We designed a robot that could open and close a locker."

Leo laughed. "That was very useful, wasn't it?"

Jim ignored him. "Then in college, that's where I really hit my stride..."

Juliet settled into her seat for the long history of James, who goes by Jim. She'd underestimated him. She thought he was going to be a silent and easily bulldozed kind of guy. It turned out that he was quiet at first because the only topic that interested him was himself. He kept talking until their entrées came.

She gave up on trying to be polite at that point. Instead, she focused on her tacos and getting the check as quickly as possible.

When they paid their checks, Sophie turned towards her with a broad smile. "We should go bowling or something. I'm not ready to go home!"

"Sorry, I can't," Juliet responded instantly. "This has been really nice, but I have a thing in the morning."

Leo shot her a smile. "What kind of thing?"

Shoot. He knew that she was lying. Did that also mean that he knew she wanted to get out of there because Jim was kind of terrible? If he worked with him, he must've known that Jim was a self-involved brown noser.

"I promised my mom I would be over in the morning," she said with resolution.

"That's too bad," said Sophie. "We should get together again soon."

"Sure," said Juliet. "It was great seeing you guys, and Jim, it was nice meeting you. Have a good night."

Juliet wasn't going to wait to make a graceful exit. She got out of there before Jim asked for her number.

Another bad date on the books. As she drove home, she repeated some of the things that Jim said and laughed out loud to herself. How could Sophie have thought she was desperate enough to date that guy? Had Sophie ever even spoken to him before?

When Juliet heard that his name was James, she was worried that it might be her James. Well, not "her" James – he wasn't hers anymore.

He was never hers, actually.

Well, whatever, she was relieved when it wasn't *that* James.

But she also felt a bit disappointed, and she wasn't sure where exactly that was coming from. She pushed it out of her mind and got ready to camp out in front of the TV for the rest of the night.

Chapter 16

Logan arranged a meeting with Kylie at a coffee shop. James was glad that she agreed to meet with him, though he felt a bit concerned that she might read into it and get the wrong idea.

When he spotted her, he remembered instantly who she was. She hadn't changed much – she had long, dyed blonde hair. She always wore fake eyelashes, which James found distracting because they were so ridiculously long. And she had on so much eye makeup that she looked like she was about to walk onto a stage somewhere.

She was a pretty woman, for sure – but definitely not his type. It wasn't personal that he didn't like her. The only woman he liked was Juliet. Maybe he should've just told her that the first time she brought in danishes.

He made sure to make it obvious that it was a professional meeting from the start. "Kylie, I'm going to cut right to the chase."

She offered a small smile. "Okay."

"Balin Labs is working on a monoclonal antibody that's a lot like one of your company's drugs – Delicaid. And I think that we could really use a great mind like yours to market it."

"Oh. That's interesting." She sat back and crossed her arms. "Our drug is just starting in human trials, though."

"Right. Ours is a few steps ahead as far as humans go, but we missed an opportunity, I think, in marketing to pet owners as well."

She scrunched her eyebrows slightly. "I'm not involved with any of the animal stuff."

Shoot. He probably should have looked into what she actually did at the company before coming up with this big fake job offer. "Of course, but you've been around it for so long, that I'm sure that you'd be a great asset."

"I see."

She didn't seem as open as he expected. Was she still mad that he didn't return her romantic advancements?

No, that would be silly. How long could she hold onto a grudge just because he didn't like her back?

James continued. "Have you been involved at all with this contest? This video contest to raise funding for veterinary clinics?"

She nodded. "Yeah, I've done work with some of that."

"Oh that's great." He didn't know how to casually ask her if she was a judge, or who the judges were, or what they were looking for. So he decided to just go for it.

"For something like that, what's the drive? Do you use all of the videos for your own promotion? What makes a video the best video? Do you contact the pet owners on your own?"

She shrugged. "It depends. I don't make those decisions though."

"Sure. Well, if you came back to work for us, you could be in charge of anything you wanted."

He was really promising the moon here. Whatever – for all he cared, she could come back and be in charge of a new marketing division. She'd be fine – probably. As long as she didn't keep bringing him boxes of baked goods.

"Thank you, but I'm very happy where I am." A smirk curled at the corner of her lips. "Let's just say that the culture at my current company is different than Balin Labs."

James frowned. "In that case, can I come and work with you?"

She laughed. "I don't think that's possible."

"A friend of mine entered the contest – that's actually how I heard about it. I was really impressed with it. The award ceremony – is it just for this one grant?"

Kylie shook her head. "No, it's just one part of the event. Our company likes to throw a party every year for all of the employees and vendors. Black tie, of course. It's a lot of fun, we also give out awards to salesman and innovators. Something I could never see happening at Balin Labs."

"That does sound really nice," James responded. "And you're right, something my dad would never go for. He'd say it was a waste of money."

Kylie smiled politely.

"Not to say that I agree with him," added James. "I think it's incredible. Truly."

"Thanks. Which is why you can understand," Kylie said, stiffening her shoulders, "why I'm not interested in leaving."

"Alright then, I had to try. Plus you gave me an idea where we could improve."

Kylie smiled. "Sure."

James stood from his seat and shook her hand. "Well, thank you for taking the time to talk to me today, if you change your mind, you know how to find me."

She stood, too. "Thank you, James. Best of luck to you."

He smiled and nodded. He wasn't sure what *that* was supposed to mean. Best of luck? With their new drug? Or finding a marketing person?

He didn't know, but she wasn't being very forthcoming about the contest and he didn't want to waste more time talking to her. He needed to fly back to Cleveland and pick up his car. He had the irresistible urge to drive back to Lansing, and he didn't want to spend another minute with Kylie if he didn't need to.

When he arrived at the car shop to pick up the Porsche, he half expected the police to spring from the bushes and arrest him. Luckily, they did not. His dad must've gotten over being mad. Or at least decided it wasn't worth endangering Balin Labs' reputation to get back at him.

James got into the Porsche and drove straight for Lansing. He'd managed to book a behind-the-scenes tour of the Lansing Zoo, and there was only one person that he wanted to take with him. The problem was that she wasn't speaking to him at the moment.

He checked into a hotel on Saturday evening. The zoo tickets were for Sunday, and he was running out of time to call Juliet and see if she'd agree to go with him. He was terrified that she was going to say no, and then he'd have to put plan B into place.

By 8 o'clock that night, he set his mind to make the phone call. She might be getting ready for bed for all he knew; he couldn't wait any longer. He took a deep breath and called her cell phone.

"Hello?"

She answered!

"Hey Juliet, it's James. How are you?"

"I'm good, how are you?"

"I'm good," he said. "I just wanted to make sure that you got home and that you didn't have any trouble with the bus."

"Nope. No problems."

Well that was stupid of him to say, because that wasn't the *only* reason he was really calling. "That's good! Glad to hear it. I wanted to, uh, also apologize for almost killing you in that car accident."

Juliet laughed. "First Deno, now me. You're developing a habit."

"I really am sorry," he stammered. "I should've listened to you. I thought I was being helpful by getting us to Cleveland more quickly, but I was really just being pigheaded."

"Well, thank you for apologizing. But it's fine – really."

He took a deep breath. "Okay, good. And just so you know, I talked to my dad. He told the police that the car wasn't stolen. He was just being, you know, petty."

"Ah. I'm glad to hear that there isn't a warrant for my arrest floating around in the world."

He laughed. "No, there is not. And actually, I wanted to make it up to you – you know, the car crash and everything. And I got these tickets for the Lansing Zoo tomorrow for a behind-the-scenes tour."

Silence.

"Are you there?" he asked.

"Yes, I'm here."

"Oh. Did you hear what I said? I wanted to see, if you have the time, and if you wanted to do a behind-the-scenes tour with me. Of the zoo."

"Tomorrow?"

"Yeah. It starts at noon, but if that doesn't work – "

"No, that would be fine."

He froze. Did she just agree to go with him?

"Noon then? We could head over a little early and walk around the zoo first?"

"Sure, that'd be nice."

"Okay, great! I could pick you up at like 11, if that works?"

"Hold on, let me check the weather forecast and make sure that it's not going to snow..."

James smiled. "Ha ha. Very funny. The joke's on you because I already checked it and it's not going to snow. And if it *is* going to snow, I rented a small tank to get us there safely."

She laughed. "Okay, 11 it is. I'll see you tomorrow."

"Okay great! See you then!"

James ended the call and stared at his phone in disbelief. Did he call the right number? Was that *really* Juliet?

He fully expected that she was going to turn him down. He even booked the animal experiences in a strategic way, so that her favorite animal (the penguins) would be at the end of the day. He planned to take pictures of himself throughout the tour so that she would eventually agree to join him.

It seemed like even that was a stretch. He never expected that she would just agree to it!

It was odd, but he decided not to question it. He had another chance to see her, and that was all that mattered. After this, the only excuse he'd have to see her would be at the award ceremony when they named the winner of the video contest.

He didn't *technically* have an invitation to the ceremony, though Logan could probably secure an invitation if needed. Ideally, Juliet would agree to take him as her date. That might be too much to ask, though. He decided to take it one step at a time.

The next morning, James made sure to leave with plenty of time to get to Juliet's apartment. He wanted to be early, partially so they wouldn't miss their first animal encounter, but also to give Juliet less time to change her mind.

He was outside of her apartment at 10:40. Juliet's landlord was walking around the property, throwing down salt on the sidewalks. At one point, he looked up and made eye contact with James.

James slowly raised his right hand and used two fingers to make a V, pointing first at his own eyes, then at the landlord. The universal "I'm watching you" hand gesture.

The landlord froze for a moment before hurriedly picking up the bucket of salt and rushing into a house next door to the building.

James laughed to himself. At least the landlord wouldn't be bothering Juliet today.

Juliet came out of the apartment building a few minutes later, dressed in hiking books and a North Face jacket. James felt his heart jump; she looked like she walked right out of a camping magazine.

"Hey," she said as she opened the car door.

James silently scolded himself for not getting out to open the door for her. Instead he gaped at her like an idiot.

"Hey, are you ready to go?"

"I think so." Her eyes scanned him from head to toe. "Are you sure you're going to be warm enough in that?"

"Oh don't worry," he said. "I have a jacket in the back seat. I can't drive wearing it, it restricts my range of motion too much."

She smiled. "That's important for making sure you don't get into an accident, right?"

"That's right," he said with a smile. "I hope you're ready for some close-up animal encounters."

"How many animals do we get to meet?"

"We have four today."

She turned towards him. "Four!"

James was glad to hear the excitement in her voice. He loved booking these encounters whenever they were offered at a zoo, and he knew Juliet would love it too.

"Yes. We've got the big cats up first – I think it'll be the African lions and the Siberian tigers. There's a snow leopard, but I'm not sure if we get to see her."

"I think they're pretty shy," Juliet said.

"Yeah, I think so too. After that, we have the black rhino."

"Oh, that'll be nice."

"And last but not least, we have the river otters and the Magellanic Penguins."

Juliet's hand shot to her mouth. "Really? Do you think we get to pet the penguins?"

James laughed. "Usually they let you, yeah. I've done three other experiences with penguins and they're pretty laid-back. There is usually at least one penguin who enjoys attention."

Juliet smiled. "I have to admit, this sounds pretty cool."

"I'm glad you think so. I figured it should mostly make up for almost killing you."

"Mostly," she said, turning back to look out of the window. "But what about your favorite animal? They don't have anything with elephants?"

"No, but I think that's because they don't have any elephants in the zoo."

"Ah, that makes sense then. I haven't been there in a long time."

"Clearly!" said James. "I can't believe you haven't done all of these experiences a couple of times already."

Juliet shrugged. "My days are pretty full with dogs, cats, pigs and horses."

"Fair enough."

James kept his eyes on the road. He just had to make sure not to mess everything up like he did last time. As long as one of the animals didn't try to eat her, what could possibly go wrong?

Chapter 17

They arrived at the zoo in no time. Juliet felt a bit silly that she agreed to go out with him. If she was being honest with herself, she felt sad when he stopped contacting her, especially after that dud of a date with the other James.

Then, when he called her out of the blue, she was so excited that she agreed to whatever he suggested. It was like all of her wry suspicion of him went out of the window and she turned into a giddy school girl.

Ugh, how embarrassing. Her cheeks burned as James found a parking spot.

At the same time, it seemed that he really might just be sorry and want to apologize for almost killing her. As far as apologies go, this was one of his best. He was always able to skillfully employ the big apology. Maybe because he often needed a big apology. Whatever the reason, he was good at it.

The zoo only had a few people milling about; even though it was a clear and beautiful day, it was bitterly cold. James suggested that they get hot cocoa to keep them warm as they walked around and Juliet agreed; James always seemed to know how to add a little luxurious touch to every situation.

With hot cocoa in hand, they decided to follow the path to the left of the entrance and take a look at the river otters. Unfortunately, the otters were nowhere to be seen.

"They're probably in the back getting ready to hang out with us," James decided.

"Right," replied Juliet. "Like they have nothing better to do."

He shrugged. "You never know. They could be back there in that cement hut, preparing appetizers for us, busting up oysters with their little rocks."

Juliet ignored the part about the otters preparing food for them. "Oysters? Do you think river otters eat oysters?"

He paused. "Maybe?"

"So you think that they swim out to the ocean, go oyster diving, and bring them back to the river?"

He tapped his chin. "When you put it that way, it doesn't sound right, does it?"

She laughed. "No, it doesn't."

"Well whatever they're eating, I know that they keep a favorite rock to bust open hard shells. For like crabs and things."

"Yeah, freshwater clams and mussels."

He pointed at her. "That's what I meant! Mussels! Not oysters."

Juliet nodded knowingly. "Right."

They moved on to the next exhibit – gray wolves. Again, they didn't see any animals in the enclosure, but James wanted to wait for a few minutes in case one of them decided to make an appearance.

"I don't think that they're going to come out and play with us just because we want them to," said Juliet.

Just then, they caught sight of movement at the far corner of the pen. A beautiful white wolf trotted across the enclosure, coming to a stop on a high rock, casually laying down and draping her paws over the front.

Juliet realized that her mouth was open. "She's magnificent."

"She is," said James.

Juliet couldn't take her eyes off of her fur, illuminated in the sunlight. "She looks so much like my old dog Ruthie."

James squinted. "Yeah, she might be a little bigger."

"Well, obviously."

"Ruthie was a German Shepherd, right?"

"Yeah. And she was pure white, like that wolf."

"I remember. Well – I remember you showing me pictures of her. She was gorgeous."

Juliet felt her chest tighten. It'd been years since Ruthie passed away from lung cancer, but even thinking about her still brought tears to her eyes.

"She was."

James turned towards her. "Please don't get upset. You gave her a good life."

"I know. It's just – it's really hard to lose a pet. You love them like family."

"Is that why," he said slowly, "you've never had another dog?"

Juliet swallowed. Why was James so nosy? "No."

She turned to walk away from him.

"I'm sorry," he called out. "I'm not trying to make you angry."

"Well you're not doing a very good job." She continued walking down the path.

James caught up to her in a moment. "Hey, I really am sorry."

She closed her eyes. It wasn't his fault that she still missed her dog. And it wasn't his fault that she was too afraid to get another dog, too afraid to love that dog for years and years and then one day, inevitably, have to say goodbye.

"No," she said, stopping. "I'm sorry for acting like that. I know it's been a long time, it's just – still a touchy subject."

"I get it," he said. "Well, not exactly. I haven't been able to have a dog. Or cat. Or even a goldfish, really."

"I know."

"My life," he said dramatically, "has been completely devoid of joy."

She laughed. "Stop it. No it hasn't."

"It's a very sad case. You know how I like to sit and cry in front of my fireplace."

"Yes yes," she said with a groan. "I know all about that. What's next? Kangaroos?"

They didn't have much time to walk around before it was time for their big cat encounter. They met with their first zookeeper, a woman named Sheila. She took them behind the scenes as she prepared meat for the tigers. Then they got to watch the tigers as they ate, not five feet away from where they stood. They were behind steel bars, of course, but it was still a thrill.

Next up, Sheila took them to the lion enclosure where they repeated the process.

"Is this going to be like one of those YouTube videos," asked James, "where the lion knows you from years ago and comes running up and wraps his big paws around your neck?"

Sheila laughed. "Definitely not. These big guys know me pretty well, but I wouldn't get between them and a cut of meat."

James leaned in to Juliet's ear. "How crazy would it be if the lion ran up and hugged *me* that way?"

"I'd be really impressed," she whispered back, "that you'd managed to keep that relationship quiet for so long."

They stood and admired the lions for the next fifteen minutes. Juliet couldn't believe how big they were close up – it would be terrifying to run into one of them in the wild.

Next up was zookeeper Ryan, who introduced them to the zoo's black rhino, Dario.

"We're going to give him a snack," said Ryan. "And then you can have a chance to pet him."

"Wait, really?" said James. "Isn't he aggressive?"

Ryan shook his head. "Nope. Dario is a gentle giant. You're going to love him."

Juliet was surprised by how sleepy and easy-going Dario was. They reached through the bars of the enclosure to pet his rough skin. He quietly munched on some vegetables, eyes half closed.

"This definitely isn't how I saw my Sunday going," said Juliet. "But I can't complain."

James smiled. "Good."

After that, they returned to the river otter exhibit. Ryan told them about the diet of a river otter, which allowed Juliet to crack many jokes at James' expense.

The otters themselves were unbelievably lovable. Juliet couldn't get over how graceful they were in the water.

They each got to feed the otters a piece of fish using a pair of tongs. The otters reached up with their adorable little paws and snatched the fish away.

At the end of the day, they got to meet the penguins. Ryan told them that the penguins were the only animals that were hand fed every day, so they too could hand feed the penguins.

"This is *amazing*," gushed Juliet as she lugged a bucket of fish into the penguin enclosure.

James sighed. "I'm pretty sure they would prefer oysters to these stinky fish."

Juliet rolled her eyes. One of the penguins waddled up to her and pecked at her shoelaces.

"Oh my gosh! Look, he likes me!"

"I don't know, I think he wants to steal your shoes."

"Don't be ridiculous," quipped Juliet. "They're not even his size."

James burst out laughing, which startled the penguin. He stopped pecking at Juliet to turn his head and look at James.

"Get out of here before you scare him away!" whispered Juliet. "You don't have a great history with birds."

James obediently shuffled backwards, and the penguin continued his pursuit of her shoelaces.

Once they ran out of fish, they thanked Ryan for showing them around and exited back onto the main zoo path.

"After being in that humid penguin exhibit," Juliet said, stuffing her hands deep into her pockets, "I don't know if I can stand being outside much longer."

"I'm so glad you said that, because I was thinking the same thing," said James. "Would you want to grab a bite to eat?"

Juliet bit her lip. She knew that she should go home. She'd spent more than enough time with James. There was no need to get too friendly with him and allow unwanted feelings to bubble up...

However, she knew that there wasn't anything for her to eat at home, and she was pretty hungry.

"Okay, where do you want to go?"

James shrugged. "Wherever. I'll let you pick, I don't know the restaurants around here."

"Hm...I know a really good deli?"

"Works for me!"

As they approached the car, James fumbled with the keys and dropped them on the ground.

"Are you okay?" she asked. "Do you need me to drive?"

He shook his head. "No, no I'm fine."

"Are you sure?"

He unlocked the car doors and they both took their seats. Juliet realized that her seat was already warm – he must've started the car from afar. A nice touch.

"I need to talk to you about something," he said.

Oh boy, here it was. He was finally going to tell her what he'd been after all this time. She turned towards him. "Okay, what?"

"I've always regretted how our relationship ended. To tell you the truth, I never stopped thinking about you."

Juliet felt her heart thundering in her chest. Where on *earth* was this coming from?

He kept talking. "I know this seems like it's out of left field, but I really enjoyed getting to hang out with you for the past week, and I know that I messed up big time with the driving, and I am really sorry about that – "

She felt like she had to interrupt him before he added anything else. "It's fine, I swear."

He flashed a brief smile. "What I'm trying to say, very poorly, is that I would love to spend more time with you. I was hoping we could go to the award ceremony together?"

"You want to go to the gala?"

"Well, yeah, with you. We could go just as friends, but what I really always wondered – I mean, what I really want is to know if you could ever consider giving me another chance?"

Juliet sat back. She definitely didn't expect this. It was hard to look at his pleading blue eyes. She looked away.

"I don't know what to say, James."

He jumped in. "Just say that we can go together, and I can see you win the funding for your clinic. And then, if I don't mess anything else up or almost kill you, you might want to see me again. And then if I don't mess anything up that time, you might want to see me again, and so on..."

How could this possibly be what he was after? She almost felt like she was back in college, the night he asked her to dinner, and she was so sure he just wanted help with biology lab or something.

"James – we broke up so long ago..."

"I know. I was a very different person then. A worse person."

Juliet felt like her head was spinning. This was too much to take in. "I don't – "

"You don't have to answer right now. I just feel like – well, I can't keep making up excuses to see you. I figured you were going to get suspicious that I was in Lansing so often."

Juliet laughed. "Yeah, I was getting a bit suspicious."

Except that she was completely off base as to what he was scheming. Why couldn't she fathom that he might still have feelings for her?

It just seemed...impossible. And arrogant, that this rich and successful guy would still be in love with her. When they broke up, she felt like he didn't even care. Not really, not enough to keep his promise to move to Texas. Not that she gave him the option, but still, he made his choice.

Was this just a case of wanting something he couldn't have?

"I know it's been a long time," he said. "But I couldn't live with myself if I didn't at least let you know how I felt about you."

She rubbed her forehead. "This is kind of a lot, James."

"I know," he said putting his hands up. "I get it. I didn't mean to dump this on you. So maybe take the week to think about it, and if you'll have me as your guest at the ceremony, we can see how it goes?"

She sighed. "I'll think about it."

"Thank you."

She cleared her throat. Time to change the subject. "Do you want the address for the deli then?"

"Sure," he responded. He seemed much less nervous after saying his piece.

It seemed that he passed his nervousness off to Juliet.

Chapter 18

They ate dinner at the deli, James regretting that he agreed to go. It wasn't because the food wasn't good, because it was – but because the service was so quick that they were done in 30 minutes. He hoped to have more time with Juliet, but before he knew it, he was dropping her off at her apartment.

He didn't want to put pressure on her, so he didn't bring up the gala again.

"Well, I hope that your zoo experience somewhat made up for me almost killing you."

She laughed. "Yeah, I think we're even."

"Great."

"That means no more wasting money on me," she added.

He gave her a shocked face. "Wasting? It's hardly a waste to have a once-in-a-lifetime experience like that."

"Uh huh."

"And besides, what's money worth anyways?"

He stopped himself before saying the second half of his catch phrase: if you can't spend it on someone you love. No need to use the L-word when she was already nervous around him.

She unbuckled her seatbelt and opened the door. "I should've *known* you were going to say that. Alright buddy, time to go home and cry in front of your fireplace."

"I will," he said with a laugh. "Have a good evening!"

"See you."

He watched as she walked back into the building. He was well aware that this may be the last time that he got to see her; being her date to the gala was really the last thing he could think of to wrench himself into her life.

At least he told her how he felt. It was finally out there. It was a relief, but it also terrified him.

To Juliet, it may have seemed like it came out of nowhere, but for him, he'd been waiting for this moment for years. If he was lucky enough to be her date, he could not mess *anything* up. If he did, she would probably never see him again.

All that there was left to do was wait for her decision. He didn't want to annoy her, so other than a few text messages back and forth about the blizzard that hit Lansing the next morning, he didn't say anything else. Instead, he tried to busy himself with making sure that he would be ready to be the best possible date.

By Thursday, James started getting nervous he hadn't heard from her. Maybe she had someone else that she wanted to take.

Why hadn't he considered that? It was highly possible that she had a bunch of guys chasing after her. James probably wasn't the only one. But he was the only one who'd broken her heart and been a terrible disappointment before.

On Friday morning, she sent a text. "Did I ever send you the final videos?"

"No, you didn't. But I'd love to see them," he responded.

She sent a link to both the long and short versions of her video entry. They were both incredible, and he even started tearing up at the end – not only because it was so touching that all of these animals and their owners went through cancer and made it, but also because it was so closely related to Juliet. This is what she did every day. She helped people take care of and save the animals that they loved.

"Those were incredible," he wrote back. "I don't know how anyone could beat you. Have you seen any of the other videos?"

"Yeah, they're also on the website. Some are pretty good."

James watched some of the competitor's videos. They weren't bad, but they weren't as good as Juliet's. He told her as much.

It took her a while to write back. Juliet wasn't one for praise. "Thanks. I guess we'll see. Are you still interested in going to this thing on Saturday?"

He wrote back immediately. "Absolutely."

It felt like it took her an eternity to answer, but it was only four minutes. "Well then – it's a date!"

At the same moment James was hit with intense joy and nervousness. He was actually getting a second chance. "Awesome. I'll pick you up Saturday, around noon? Let me take care of the travel, pretty please?"

"Ha, alright. I guess that's your department. See you then."

James already chartered a jet for a flight from Lansing to Chicago on Saturday. It'd be relatively quick – only an hour – but James wanted to be sure that they had enough time to outrun any storms that might cause issues.

He stayed in contact with his pilot that week to make sure they kept a close eye on the weather patterns. Luckily, it looked like Saturday would be a clear day from Lansing all the way to Chicago.

James arrived at Juliet's apartment promptly at 12 o'clock on Saturday. He no longer had the Porsche – he drove back to New York

City and left it for his dad. Instead, he bought a Subaru for their short trip to the airport.

It was the first thing that Juliet commented on.

"You're finally starting to remember what you need to survive the Michigan winter."

"I didn't want to take any chances."

"We're only going to have about two hours of leeway before the gala starts, so we'd better get going."

James reversed out of the parking spot. "About that..."

She turned to him. "What?"

"Well, I didn't think you'd want to take the risk of driving with me again..."

"James," she said flatly, "what are you up to?"

"Nothing!" he said in a too-high voice. "I just thought it would be faster, and safer, if we flew. Plus we'd have more time to get ready."

"James – "

He interrupted her. "You have to admit that a one hour flight with a real pilot is much safer than a four hour drive with me at the wheel."

She threw her hands up. "That's not the point!"

"Then what is the point?"

"Well I can't think of it right now," Juliet said, clicking her tongue, "but I'm sure I have a good one."

He laughed. "Come on, you have to admit that driving all the way there puts us at risk for missing the gala entirely."

She sighed. "I guess so."

"And although this car could get us there, do we *really* want to risk you not being able to accept the award in person?"

"If I'd have known that you were going to spend a bunch of money on a flight – "

James waved a hand. "But you didn't! I was going to do it anyways. The jet was parked in Lansing all week. I had to get it moving."

"A *jet*? James, this – "

"Listen," he said, suppressing a smile, "I'm trying to milk the perks from the company before I get fired. Is that so wrong?"

She laughed. "You'll never get fired."

"You'd be surprised."

She looked at him, as though searching his face to see if he was telling the truth.

He kept driving.

They got to the small airport and parked the car. Luckily, their flight was the only one scheduled for the next two hours, so the jet was already waiting on the runway.

James hopped out of the car, making sure to get both his and Juliet's bags. He knew she would act like it annoyed her that he carried her bag, but deep down she'd secretly appreciate it. She'd told him as much years ago and he never forgot.

They walked onto the jet and James loaded their bags into storage. As he shut the door to the baggage compartment, he stole a glance at her. She was looking around the cabin, gently touching the soft leather seats.

Juliet would never admit that she was impressed, and James didn't want her to. But it *had* to beat the bus rides that she used to take back in the day.

"Can I get you something to drink? Or a snack?" he asked.

She shook her head. "No, I'm okay. Thank you."

"Okay, I guess I'll have to drink all of these ginger ales by myself..."

She smiled. "Well I guess one ginger ale couldn't hurt."

"Coming right up!"

The flight was quick, and James spent the time looping through the other videos in the competition and making fun of them.

"Look at this. Look how shaky this image is. I'm getting motion sickness just looking at it. There's no way this one's going to beat you."

"I'm not worried about that one," said Juliet. "I'm worried about the one where they used that dolphin as a spokesperson. Er, spokes-dolphin."

James frowned. "Everyone loves Flipper. But that was all they had: one dolphin and two cats. And they had that lady droning on about how special this dolphin was for like three minutes. Way too boring."

"We'll see," said Juliet. "I thought that all of the videos were really nice."

"Aw come on," he said. "Where's your competitive spirit? We're going to blow the rest of these guys out of the water!"

"I hope not literally! I do like dolphins!"

James shrugged. "Whatever it takes to win."

"Oh my goodness," Juliet said, rubbing her forehead. "You're going to have to stay on the plane while I go to the gala. I can't allow you to threaten any of the animals in the competitor's videos."

"No, don't!" he said. "I would never! I was just kidding."

She crossed her arms. "You'd better be kidding. That's not funny."

"Okay, I'm sorry. Please don't kick me out of the gala already. I have one more surprise that I think you might actually like."

"James! What is it with you and all the surprises? You know that I don't like – "

He held his hands up. "I know, but this was necessary. It's going to be helpful."

"Please don't tell me you did something cheesy like rent a limo to take us there."

He almost did, but the image of her disgusted face flashed into his mind and he abandoned the idea. "No, nothing like that."

"Then what is it?"

He bit his lip. "Do you really want to know? Don't you want to just be surprised?"

"Not really, don't make me turn this plane around!"

"Please don't do that," James said, a smile tugging at his lips. "Okay, listen. I'm not going to tell you what the surprise is, because you really need to see it to understand it. But I promise that I only did it because I really thought that you would like it and appreciate it, and it's the last one. I swear."

Juliet hid her face in her hands. "Why do I have a bad feeling about this?"

He laughed. "Probably because I get a lot of bad ideas. But! You'll find out soon, and you can judge for yourself."

"Ugh, fine." She put her hands up in defeat. "Did you say that you had snacks?"

James smiled. She was finally giving him a little bit of trust. He had to make sure not to overdo it.

"Yes, I did. Let me go and grab them."

Chapter 19

The plane started its descent into Chicago. Juliet made sure that her seatbelt was fastened as she nervously munched on some pretzels. She hoped that they would settle her stomach, but nothing was helping. She couldn't get over the feeling that she was in over her head.

She spent days agonizing over whether she should take James as her date to the gala. It wasn't just that James wanted to be her date – that she could've stomached. It was more than that. He asked her to give him *another chance*.

Why did he have to say it out loud like that? Even if taking him as her date meant that she was giving him another chance, she didn't like thinking of it that way. It made her feel too...vulnerable.

She made the mistake of seeking advice from Aaron and Greg, and the first thing that Greg did was gloat.

"I knew it! I knew that he still liked you!"

"And you don't seem to despise him either," added Aaron.

They were doing a video chat but Juliet wasn't sure if they could make out the dirty look she was giving them. "I don't still like him."

"Then why did you agree to drive around with him for a week?" asked Aaron.

"I had no choice! My car was broken down!"

"Uh huh," said Aaron. "Like there was no other option. And you hated every minute of it."

She sighed. "I mean, he did almost kill the first pet we went to see. And he almost killed me, too. But other than that, it wasn't all bad."

"See how much fun you can have," said Greg. "when you forgive and forget?"

"So you're saying to forget about him," quipped Juliet. "I think you're right."

Greg shook his head. "No, that's not what I'm saying. I'm saying that if you like him, and if you think it's worth giving him another chance, you should."

"It's not that easy!" said Juliet.

Aaron shrugged. "It kind of is. Plus, it's not like you've dated a bunch of other guys after you broke up with him."

"Yeah," agreed Greg, "we decided that he's kinda like your one true love."

"Very funny guys," said Juliet. They were more interested in teasing her than helping her. "I have to go, talk to you later, I *guess.*"

"Bye!" they said at the same time.

She ended the call. What did she expect to get from them? Of course they were going to crack jokes.

James as her one true love – how ridiculous. It was true that she hadn't had any success in dating after she broke up with him, but it was partially because she didn't try very hard.

And that may have been because breaking up with him shattered her heart into a million pieces, and it takes a long time to recover from something like that. She didn't want to just jump into a relationship with a new guy when her heart was still in tatters.

It just turned out that she never got around to finding that new guy. Or fully repairing her heart. And now, she followed that confused heart of hers all the way onto a private jet.

"Do you want to go into the cockpit for landing?" asked James. "It's pretty cool to see."

Now *that* was something that could distract her from eating every last pretzel on the plane. "Sure."

She followed him up to the cockpit and he introduced her to Gary, the pilot. Gary invited her to sit in the copilot chair and put on a headset.

She was dazzled by the view – it was breathtaking to see the city from so high above.

"This is incredible!" she said.

"Go ahead," said Gary, "take the wheel!"

She raised her hands up and far away from the controls. "Absolutely not!"

James and Gary laughed.

The plane landed with a delicate touch onto the runway.

"This doesn't look like an international airport," commented Juliet. It was a tad busier than the airport in Lansing, but not by much.

"It's not," said James. "It's a regional airport. But don't worry, we have a car taking us to the hotel."

"Bring the car around," she said, nose in the air.

He smiled. "I told you, I don't think I have very long to enjoy this. And I'd just like to share it with you."

Her stomach leapt; she felt caught off guard by his sincerity. "I don't know why you keep saying that."

"It's a long story. But I don't want it to spoil the night."

She didn't press for any more details and instead made her way down to the car waiting on the tarmac. James rushed to open the door for her, which she thought was silly, but she decided not to say anything.

"Are we going to the Tiffany Suites again?" she asked.

"Of course," he said.

She bit her lip. Even though she didn't have the money in her bank account to cover hotel rooms, she didn't want James to think that she was some sort of a mooch, or that she owed him anything.

"Well then, I insist on paying this time."

"I'm afraid that won't be possible," he said.

She crossed her arms. "I mean it!"

"I do too," he said, cracking a smile. "It was a last-minute thing and they only had rooms for Gold Star members. And I have to pay for that in points."

"Fine then," Juliet said. "I'll pay you for the points."

"They don't really have a dollar value," said James. "And if you can believe it, this is the last of my points, so who cares!"

"*They don't really have a dollar value*," scoffed Juliet. "I'm sure that I can look up the rate of a room."

She pulled out her phone to find the hotel's website.

"I'd prefer you didn't do that," said James.

"Why?" she said, typing in a date for the room. "Do you think I can't afford it?"

He frowned. "No, it's not that."

The price finally loaded on her screen: nearly $700 a night. For single room! Her jaw dropped. That was even more ridiculous than she imagined.

"What? How much is it?" asked James.

She shoved her phone back in her purse. "You have no idea how much this hotel costs, do you?"

"Of course I do...in points."

She let out an exaggerated sigh. "If you're going to get fired from your dad's company soon, you need to get better with your money. Let me book us rooms at a more reasonable hotel."

"No can do, Juliet. Your surprise is already set up for you in your room."

Why was he so persistent? "I told you, no more surprises."

"You know about this one already, so it isn't a *new* surprise, it's an old surprise that you haven't gotten yet."

She laughed. Though she didn't want to admit it, she was curious to see what this was. "Okay buddy. Just don't push your luck."

He flashed her a cheesy smile. "I would never."

They got to the hotel and the staff immediately ran to get their bags. They were acting like they were royalty or something. Normally Juliet would be embarrassed by this sort of a show, but for some reason, today she just decided to go with it.

She never liked acting fancy, but James clearly didn't get the memo. She didn't want to fight him at every turn. What was the point? She'd already agreed to this absurd date.

Plus, it seemed that the one day that it would be appropriate to feel fancy would be the day she went to a gala. It was probably the only gala she would ever go to in her life.

They were immediately escorted to their rooms. Juliet opened the door to hers slowly, poking her head inside. She was afraid that a bunch of parrots would fly out or something.

Nothing seemed out of place at first, except that the room was very large. It truly was a suite, complete with two bedrooms, a living room, and a kitchen. She took a few steps into the living room and gasped.

Inside were three tall racks filled with floor-length gowns. She stepped forward, lightly touching the fabric of one of the brilliantly colorful dresses.

"Now before you get angry at me and say that you already have a dress picked out and that you know how to dress yourself," stammered James, "these are simply an option and if you don't want them I'll send them back to – "

"They're beautiful. They're so beautiful."

Relief washed over James' face. "Really? Okay, good! Well, feel free to try all of them on. I have a team of seamstresses waiting in the next room over to help adjust whichever dress you choose."

Juliet couldn't pull her eyes away from the cascading fabrics. "Thank you."

With that, he tiptoed backwards out of the room and closed the door softly. Juliet blushed – he must be afraid that she was going to snap on him. Was she really *that* bad?

She'd felt very self-conscious about the dress that she wrestled out of the back of her closet for this event. While she wanted something nice to wear, she just didn't have the time or the energy to find something.

This surprise was actually perfect. Well, maybe it was a bit too much – especially with that team of seamstresses – but it was the thought that counted.

The old James might've had a similar idea, but he would've done it in an entirely different way. He would've brought her to a fancy designer store where she felt uncomfortable and the pressure from the salespeople made her self-conscious. He would've insisted that she pick one, not give her the option.

Perhaps James matured and really was new and improved, and this wasn't a huge mistake after all?

Chapter 20

Amazing – she actually seemed happy! Not that James planned for her not to like the surprise, but in the past, he always seemed to do things in the wrong way. It seemed that he finally understood what was and was not acceptable to her.

James intended to leave her in peace as she got ready for the gala. As for himself, all he needed to do was to shower and put on his tuxedo.

He didn't want to get ready too early and risk wrinkling the tux, so instead, he sat on the couch and tried to watch TV. He was too nervous to actually get engaged with anything, but it was something to pass the time.

His mind wandered and he pulled out his phone to glance at his email – there were over 200 emails from work that he was ignoring. He put his phone away without reading any of them.

A few days ago, a feeling of dread washed over him when he real-ized that he'd have to answer them eventually. His dad was likely still angry at him, and James didn't know what the point of it all was.

Was he really going to go back to New York and keep fighting with his dad? Someone else should take his position – from what his dad said, anyone could do a better job than he did.

That was when an idea hit him: James could just never go back.

It wasn't that he felt bitter about the job – not anymore at least. Nothing about it mattered to him anymore. Being away from the city and from the other employees of the company really opened his eyes. The rest of the world didn't revolve around quarterly earnings and sales projections. People didn't work from six in the morning until ten o'clock at night, trying to out-stay each other at the office to make themselves look the hardest working.

What made him laugh now was the realization that his job wasn't anything important. He wasn't an actual scientist, testing the drugs. He wasn't helping people, like Juliet did. He was a salesperson, often times trying to convince others that one of their expensive drugs was better than it was. It was a waste of time for everyone involved.

No matter what happened with Juliet, even if she decided that she had no interest in seeing him again, he couldn't go back to living that life. He had to do something better.

With about 30 minutes before they had to leave for the gala, James hopped in the shower and put on his tux. He didn't want to rush Juliet, but he wanted to give her a warning about the time.

James approached her door quietly, trying to hear if there was any commotion inside. He could hear nothing. He knocked softly, and one of the seamstresses opened the door by just a crack.

"Hello," he said. "Just wanted to let Juliet know that we have about ten minutes before we should leave."

"I'm ready to go," called out Juliet's voice from behind the door. "You can come in."

James smiled and walked into the suite. "Did you find anything you liked?"

Juliet stepped out of one of the bedrooms, a royal blue dress gracefully framing her figure. "Yeah, I think so!"

It was like the wind was knocked out of him. He always thought Juliet was a beautiful woman, usually running from one place to the next in her jeans and hiking boots. She didn't like getting dressed up, though, so it was rare to see her like this.

She was breathtaking. She was more beautiful than any woman he'd seen in New York City – and he was pretty sure that he once saw Angelina Jolie getting into a car in Manhattan.

"You look – "

She interrupted him. "Like a winner, right? That's why I picked the blue one. So they can pin the blue ribbon on me."

James laughed and shook his head. "Ah, of course. Yes, you look like an absolute winner."

"Thank you," she said, walking past him. "You look pretty dapper yourself. Are you ready to do this thing?"

"Yes, definitely. Let's go."

They walked down to the lobby and got into their (non-limo) ride. James had a hard time not staring at Juliet and instead tried pointing out of the window to show her different areas of Chicago that he knew. She didn't say much; James wondered if perhaps she was nervous.

They arrived at the gala and rushed inside. It was too cold to be loitering outside, and besides, there was a sort of indoor red carpet for taking pictures. James checked both of their coats and joined Juliet on the red carpet.

"This seems a bit silly," said Juliet in a low voice.

"Of course it is," said James. "But it's fun. Look how much people are enjoying it. My dad would never go for something like this for our company – he'd say it was a waste of money."

Juliet shrugged. "It probably is."

A woman holding a camera with a long lens approached them. "Would you two like a picture?"

Juliet started to shift away, but James placed his hand gently on the side of her waist to pull her in.

"I would love a picture," he said.

Juliet gave him the side eye, but obliged in posing.

"Thanks!" said the photographer. "They'll be on the website later this week."

James thanked her, and Juliet insisted on pressing forward so that no one else would try to take their picture. They made it to the front entrance where two women were checking names off of the guest list.

Juliet stepped forward to the woman on the left.

"Hi there. Name?" asked the woman.

"Juliet McCarron."

The woman peered over her glasses at James. "And this must be your Romeo?" she said with a laugh.

Juliet laughed politely, but James knew that was one of her least favorite jokes from back when they were dating.

The second woman turned away from the couple that she'd been helping and set her eyes on them.

"No, that's not Romeo," she said cooly. "That's James Balin."

James froze and turned to look at the owner of that familiar voice.

"Oh, hi Kylie," he said. "I didn't see you there."

She flashed a smile. "Good to see you again."

The first woman checked off a name on her list. "I see you right here, Juliet. And I have this rose for you to thank you for your entry and for being a finalist in our Delicaid competition."

Juliet accepted the rose with a smile. "Thank you."

The woman continued. "Dinner is just about to begin. Your award ceremony will be held in ballroom A, and that is where you'll

find your seats. Don't forget to explore the other ballrooms for dancing, games and exhibits!"

Juliet nodded. "Thank you so much."

James cleared his throat. "Thank you ladies."

Kylie smiled broadly at him. "Have a lovely night James."

When they reached the ballroom, Juliet turned to him and
asked, "How did you know that woman?"

"Oh," he said, scratching the back of his neck. "She used to work
at our company. If you couldn't tell, she didn't love it there."

"I could tell," said Juliet. "Shall we find our seats?"

"Sure."

They were seated at a long table with all of the other finalists.
James recognized some of them and immediately set his mind to
avoid any pleasantries. Unfortunately, Juliet had the opposite idea.
She introduced herself to everyone, then brought up thoughtful
compliments for each video.

It was such a Juliet thing to do. James would've preferred to treat
them all like strangers – or better yet, the competitors that they were.
He didn't need to make friends with these people.

Juliet noticed his sour attitude; she waited until the salads were
served to elbow him in the ribs. "Could you be a little less hostile?"

He shrugged. "No. But I could be *more* hostile."

"You know, all of these people want the same thing that I do.
They want to help animals. And they also need the money for their
clinics. I can't say that mine is any more deserving than theirs are."

James looked around the table. Everyone was chatting pleasantly.
He felt his heart fall. "I guess I didn't think of it that way."

She smiled and took a big bite of her bread roll. "You need to
stop being so..."

"So what?" he asked, leaning in.

She took a sip of water. "I don't know exactly. So like your dad, I guess? So...vicious."

"Now that is truly shocking!" he said, covering his mouth with his hand. "I can't believe you just said that."

Laughing, she grabbed his hand to pull away from his mouth. "Oh stop. You know what I mean. You're being very – competitive."

He continued his mock outrage, pretending to pull his hand away so she had to hold onto it longer. "Well yeah! I want you to win!"

She winked. "Okay James."

Their entrées were served, and James made an effort to talk to the people around him. Juliet was right, as always. They were all very nice and sincere, trying to win funding for worthy causes. Once Juliet finished her dessert, though, he leaned in to whisper in her ear.

"I'll give it to you that these people are nice, but please get me away from them before I do something crazy like praise their work."

"What do you suggest?" she asked. "We could go and look at one of the ballrooms with exhibits and – "

James waved a hand. "No, nothing like that. What about the ballroom with dancing?"

Juliet sat back, lightly placing a hand on her stomach. "I don't think that I can dance after all the food that I just ate."

James offered his hand to her. "Can you at least try?"

She looked away and laughed. He didn't budge. Finally, she took his hand.

"Alright, let's see what you've got," she said.

Chapter 21

Walking hand-in-hand with James made Juliet feel tingly all over. What on earth was she doing! Two weeks ago she was living her regular, boring life. The only thing she was worried about was getting funding for the clinic. And now?

Now she was at a black tie event, dressed in an evening gown like she was some sort of debutante. She giggled to herself even thinking of the word.

"What's so funny?" asked James.

"Nothing," Juliet responded. And after a moment, she added, "And also everything. Everything about this is just – it's just too much."

James led her onto the dance floor. "Try not to worry so much. Let's try to enjoy the band's interpretation of The Shirelles."

"Oh!" exclaimed Juliet. "I love this song!"

James placed his right hand at a respectful height on her waist. She kept her right hand in his left, and placed her left hand on his shoulder.

"I picked up some dancing skills over the last few years," he said, starting to move to the music.

Juliet laughed. "I still haven't."

She tried to relax her muscles and follow his lead. It did seem like he knew what he was doing.

"Did you learn this by going to a bunch of fancy events all the time?" asked Juliet.

James cringed. "Kind of? I mean, I don't go to fancy events often. But if someone *has* to go to a fancy event, you know that my dad isn't going to go."

"I can see that," said Juliet just before James delicately extended her arm so she could do a spin.

She spun around and closed her eyes, then promptly crashed into him.

"Sorry!" she said. She opened her eyes to look up at him. He was laughing and clutching her hand close to his chest.

His chest was *just* like she remembered it, and she felt herself beginning to blush after remembering the last time she ran into him. Juliet pushed herself away.

"It's no problem," he said.

The song ended, and Juliet pulled away from him. They didn't need to be dancing all night – one dance was surely enough.

"Thanks," she said, clearing her throat. She turned to walk away from the dance floor and almost walked into a man who was standing behind her.

"My apologies," he said. "Are you Juliet McCarron?"

"Yes, I am."

The man extended his hand. "It's so nice to meet you, my name is Frank Schwartz. I have to tell you that I loved your entry into the Delicaid competition."

A blush fully filled Juliet's cheeks. "Oh my gosh, thank you so much. It's so nice to meet you, Frank!"

"It's very nice to meet you as well. Enjoy the rest of your evening."

"Thank you!"

James appeared behind her. "What was that about?"

"I don't know. He said he liked the video."

James nodded. "I bet he's one of the judges. I bet you won."

Juliet rolled her eyes. "Oh please. Don't get my hopes up."

"What?" he said. "I mean it. How did he know who you were?"

"I guess because I'm in part of the video explaining how the drug works."

"Oh that's right," said James. "Well it sounds like they've got a little bit of a Black Eyed Peas song going now. And I don't think I was the worst dance partner that's ever existed, so I feel like, just maybe, you might want to dance to this as well?"

Juliet looked around. "I don't know, it seems like it'd be pretty hard to dance to."

James again extended his hand. "Can I give it a shot?"

She really shouldn't be dancing with him so much. She should be...talking about medications or something.

He smiled. "Please?"

She sighed and placed her hand in his. "Okay, one more. Let's see what you've got."

After three more songs, Juliet started to feel nervous that they might miss the award ceremony back in their ballroom, so they left the dance floor and went back to their seats. It seemed that the award ceremony was just about to begin.

First, the president of the company spoke, talking about the direction of the company and his vision for the future.

James leaned in to whisper in Juliet's ear. "He's got a much sunnier outlook than we do at Balin Labs."

"Perhaps you could learn something," responded Juliet.

The first awards that were given out were to employees of the company – some of them were serious, like "Most Selfless Team

Member." Others were not so serious, like the woman who won an award for "Stinkiest Lunch."

"I would like to thank my frozen broccoli for winning me this award," she said through laughter. "I couldn't have done it without you."

After about 35 minutes of those types of awards and speeches, it was finally time to award the Delicaid winner. The president first talked about how touching all of the entries were and how honored he was to be in charge of the company that was saving so many animals' lives. Juliet felt herself tearing up.

He introduced the woman who was going to name the contest winner. She approached the microphone with an envelope in hand.

Juliet leaned to whisper in James' ear. "Isn't that your friend Kylie?"

"I wouldn't call her a friend," he said in a low voice.

Juliet turned to look at him. His skin was unusually pale and he was staring at the podium with wide eyes.

"Are you okay?" she asked.

Without looking away, he answered, "Yes. I'm fine. Just – you know, nervous."

Juliet nodded before turning back to look at the podium.

"We had over 50 entries into our contest this year, and they were all wonderful. I wish that each and every one could win," said Kylie. The crowd responded with a round of applause.

"It was a difficult decision, but the winner of the Delicaid competition and funding is..."

Juliet felt like there was a frantic toad in her chest. She couldn't look away.

"Gracie Williams from Long Island! The funding will go to the South Rock Memorial Veterinary Oncology Institute."

Gracie stood up from the table with a squeal and made her way to the front. Juliet could feel James' hand on her shoulder, but she couldn't look at him. She stared forward, clapping fiercely.

She didn't want to look like she was unhappy for Gracie. Of course she was happy for her – the program that she was running was amazing. And her video was good too. In fact, it must've been the best. Juliet kept clapping until Gracie reached the podium to give a brief speech.

Juliet sat with a smile plastered on her face. She didn't want to look like a sore loser, and it was nothing personal. She felt nauseous, though, because she knew what this meant. There was no chance that the clinic would be able to keep its doors open into the new year.

Over the next coming weeks, they would have to inform all of their clients of their soon-to-be closure. Juliet felt empty – she always knew it was a long shot, but she was still hopeful. She thought that if she gave it her all that she could actually do something good.

Unfortunately, life didn't agree with her plans.

Gracie finished her speech and tried to make her way back to their table, but she was swarmed with people who wanted to congratulate her.

Juliet stood up, ready to leave the party. James followed her lead.

"Juliet – I'm so, so sorry," he said.

She offered a weak shrug. "It's okay. I knew it was unlikely that we'd win, I just thought..."

She didn't know what she thought. She was embarrassed to admit that she thought she was going to win. It seemed so arrogant now.

Kylie appeared next to them. "Hello James."

He startled. "Oh, hey Kylie. Great work up there."

She smiled but in an instant, the smile was gone. "Thank you. And Juliet?"

"Yes?"

"You really were one of the strongest videos that we saw."

Juliet smiled. "Thank you. That means a lot."

She continued. "It's just too bad that you didn't list your association with Balin Labs in your disclosure. We had to disqualify you, of course."

Juliet's eyes darted between Kylie and James. "What?"

"She's not associated with Balin Labs," said James. "I told you, she's just a friend."

Kylie smiled longer this time. "Sorry, rules are rules. Enjoy your evening!"

Juliet stared at the table, trying to process what she just heard.

"I don't know where she got that idea," said James.

She looked up at him. "When did you tell her that I was your friend?"

"Oh, you know how these things are, sometimes when you run into people..." He stammered through his words.

"James. When could you possibly have run into her? Have you been in Chicago in the last week?"

"Well, yes – but that was only because I was trying to find out more about what the judges wanted."

She stared at him. Find out what the judges *wanted*? And he thought he could just casually get that information? From some woman who clearly disliked him?

What an idiot. She didn't know what to say; she could feel herself getting angry and she wanted to be away from the stupid ball-room.

Juliet walked as quickly as she could to the exit. James came after her, catching her on the now empty red carpet.

"Please, wait!" said James. "I can explain."

Juliet spun around. "You can explain? Tell me what you're going to explain James. Because from what I can tell, you completely ruined my chance of winning this competition. You doomed my clinic to be closed, all because you were trying to cheat."

"I wasn't trying to cheat, I was – "

"It doesn't matter!" she yelled. "This is so you. I don't know what I was expecting, I don't even know why I'm surprised anymore!"

"I didn't know that Kylie was going to do that."

"Of course. Let me guess, it's not your fault?"

He frowned. "That's not really fair."

"You know what's not fair? It's not fair that my clinic is the only place my clients can afford to take their pets, and it'll be closed forever in a few weeks."

"I know, and I'm so sorry – "

She knew that she should walk away. But she couldn't stop herself. "This is what I deserve for giving you another chance. Have you ever wondered why we broke up? Did it ever cross your mind to ask why I wouldn't marry you?"

"Of course I know why. And that's why I came back, because – "

"Because everything is always about you, James. Even when you proposed to me, you did it in a way that *you* wanted. You thought you could throw an expensive ring at me and I wouldn't ask questions about your broken promises."

He gaped at her. She couldn't stop. She didn't care if she was yelling.

"I knew it then and I know it now – I could never marry a man that only cares about himself. You never think about how your actions affect anyone else, and you never will. Excuse me, I'm going home."

Juliet stormed out of the building, leaving her coat behind. She didn't care. She just wanted to get out of there and never see his face again.

Chapter 22

As much as he wanted to follow her, James knew better. Instead, he stood on that stupid red carpet and watched her leave.

He'd finally done it. He drove the last nail into their relationship's coffin, ensuring that Juliet could never forgive him.

He had the urge to find Kylie so he could get back at her. He wanted to say something hurtful, like telling her that the reason he never wanted to eat danishes with her was because she had no class and she was petty and small-minded.

He almost walked back to the ballroom to find her, but then he stopped himself. Juliet was right – he was only thinking of himself. He was only thinking of how good it would feel for him to say something mean. It wasn't going to help Juliet and it wasn't going to help her clinic. And it wasn't Kylie's fault that Juliet was disqualified – no, that rested on James' shoulders.

He wandered back towards their table, hoping that maybe Juliet forgot something and he could return it to her as an excuse to talk. He went back to look at their spots – nothing was there.

"Is everything okay?" asked a voice behind him.

He turned around to see Gracie standing there, looking nervous.

"Oh yes," he said. "Everything's fine. Congratulations on the win, you did a great job."

"Is Juliet upset?" asked Gracie, pressing her hands together. "That she didn't win?"

"Oh my goodness, no!" said James. "Our little – uh, argument wasn't about that. Unfortunately we have what you might call...a tumultuous history."

Gracie smiled, relief evident on her face. "Oh! Okay."

James rubbed his forehead. "I've messed up with her a lot of times. But I think this might've been my final chance."

"Aw," Gracie patted him on the shoulder, "I'm sure it can't be that bad."

"Yeah, I don't know," said James with a laugh. How could he have been so stupid? This was literally the *third* time he sabotaged Juliet's project.

First he almost killed the bird. Then he almost killed her. And now, he killed her chances of winning.

"Well," continued Gracie, "if she was upset about not winning this competition, I know of at least two other competitions that she might be able to enter."

James turned to her, his back straightening. "Really? Do you know what the deadlines are?"

She nodded. "One is in March, and the other one is in June."

"Oh." His voice fell. "I don't think that'll work. I mean – I'm sure she'd be interested in entering. I just know that her clinic will run out of funding in a few weeks."

Gracie frowned. "I'm so sorry to hear that."

"Are they all for cancer drugs?"

She shook her head. "One is for a cancer drug. The other one is for diabetes."

He raised an eyebrow. "Really?"

She nodded. "Yeah. We don't have a ton of approved treatments for animals with diabetes. What's great – and terrifying – about being a veterinarian is that we can use a lot of medications that are approved for humans."

"Yeah, ones that were approved for animals too, right?"

Gracie shook her head. "No. If a drug is approved in humans, we can use it in an animal, even if there's no approved treatment in animals. It's considered an extra-label use."

"So if I had a cancer drug that was approved in humans, then Juliet could use it in her patients?"

"Yeah," she said. "I mean, there's no guarantee that it would work in animals. Every species is different and they might have different targets for the disease, or they might metabolize the drug differently."

"Delicaid worked for basically every species you could think of."

Gracie nodded. "That's because Delicaid's target is expressed in cancer regardless of species. Well, that's what we've seen so far at least."

"Right, right," said James. "But it's not approved in humans."

"Not yet. They're working on that. And it has a conditional license in animals."

James didn't know what that meant, but he sort of didn't care. He felt an idea coming to him.

"So my company has a similar medication to Delicaid. It's almost approved for the treatment of lymphoma – for people, that is."

"Is it chemotherapy?" asked Gracie.

James shook his head. "No. It's like Delicaid – a, uh, mononuclear body?"

"Hm," said Gracie. "A monoclonal antibody?"

James pointed to her. "That's it! Sorry, I'm a salesman, not a scientist. And I don't sell that drug."

"That sounds interesting, though."

"Maybe we could develop a program to use this medication in animals. That could be huge, right?"

Gracie put her hands up. "I mean, I feel like you're getting a bit ahead of yourself – I can't really speak to if it would even work or – "

James grabbed one of her hands to shake it. "You've been a huge help. Thanks Gracie."

"You're welcome?" she replied.

James walked away, pulling his cell phone out of his pocket. It was Saturday, so he didn't want to bother Logan or anyone that he knew wasn't already working. He took a chance and dialed the work phone of one of his friends who was a scientist at Balin.

"Hello, Brad speaking."

Bingo. "Hey Brad, I had a feeling you'd be working."

He laughed. "You know me too well."

"I've got a kind of crazy idea, if you have a second?"

"Sure. What's up?"

"Do you think you could help me understand more about how Tremibade works?"

"Uh, sure. Why?"

"I think we should make it available to use in animals."

"Ah," said Brad. "Well, it was tested in dogs and rabbits initially before it went on to human trials."

James cringed. He still didn't like to imagine drug testing on anyone – human or animal. "And it worked?"

"Yeah, that's how we got it approved to test in humans."

"Perfect. I'm going to fly into town tomorrow. Want to do lunch?"

Chapter 23

When Juliet stormed outside, she didn't expect their driver Reggie to spot her and pull around so quickly.

"Are you ready to go miss?" he asked through an open window.

She realized that her taking the car would strand James at the gala. Perfect.

"Yes, would you mind taking me to the hotel?"

"Of course not," he said, motioning to open his door.

"No, please, it's okay – I can let myself in. Thanks Reg."

She got into the back seat, looking over her shoulder to be sure James hadn't followed her.

She slid into the backseat and let out a sigh. She couldn't process her emotions. It was still too fresh for her to examine, so instead she pushed it out of her mind.

What she did know was that she couldn't stand to look at James again, especially if he tried to come by with some big apology. She felt trapped, though. She had no way of getting back home to Lansing.

Except...there was *one* way to get home.

She made a call to Greg.

He answered on the first ring. "Hey sister, how's it hanging? Did we win?"

"Hey Greg," she replied. "No, we didn't."

He groaned. "I'm sorry Jules."

"Please, don't be," she said. "You did an amazing job editing the videos. And it's really not your fault. It was James' fault."

"Oh come on," said Greg with a laugh. "He isn't *that* bad. You can't blame everything on him all the time."

Juliet realized she was clenching her jaw and forced herself to relax.

"Yes I can, because apparently, he met with someone from the company last week to try to cheat. He wanted to find out what the judges were looking for in the competition."

Greg was silent for a moment before responding. "Okay, that is pretty bad. But are you sure that's why you lost?"

"I can't be sure," she said quickly. She could feel her heart rate beginning to pick up again as she thought about it. "But the person who announced the winner personally came over to tell me that I was disqualified. She said that I should have disclosed that I was associated with Balin Labs."

"Ah," he said. "That all sounds...bad."

"Yeah. And now I'm stuck in Chicago with James, despite the very inconvenient fact that I never want to see him again."

"Right," replied Greg. "He's dead to me, too."

Juliet let out a big breath. "It's a mess. Anyways, Greg, I hate to ask this of you, but does Kerry still get those standby tickets from the airline that she works for?

"She does!"

"Is there any way that I could use one of them to get a flight back to Lansing? Or Detroit?"

Greg didn't hesitate. "Definitely. We have so many of those, and I've been begging you to use one for years."

Juliet laughed. "I was waiting until I really needed it."

"Clearly. Okay, give me a few minutes and I'll find out if there any open seats. When do you want to go?"

"As soon as possible."

"Alright then," he replied in an airy tone. "Let me call you back in a bit."

"Thanks so much Greg. I really appreciate it."

She arrived at the hotel and asked Reggie if he would mind waiting for her while she packed her things.

"I'm at your service," he said. "Please take your time."

Why was he so nice? "Thank you, I'll be right back."

A hotel employee rushed to open the door for her, saying, "Welcome back Mrs. Balin."

Mrs. Balin! Did James put her down as his *wife*? It didn't matter. Whatever.

"Hi, how are you?"

"I'm doing very well. Is there anything that I can do for you?"

"No, thank you. I'm just heading back to my room."

"Very good Miss."

She paused. "Actually, I think I may have lost my key."

"I can help with that," he said, darting to the front desk to have another key printed.

Juliet stifled a laugh. This was all so ridiculous. The dress, the driver, all of these people acting like she was important.

She wasn't important. She didn't even have enough money to rent a car to drive home. She *definitely* didn't have enough money to stay at this hotel, and she failed achieving the one single goal that she set for herself.

The employee handed her a new key. "Is there anything else that I can get for you?"

"No, thank you. You've been very helpful."

She got into the elevator, feeling a bit scattered, as though James could appear at any moment. Surprisingly, he hadn't tried to call or text her. Maybe he didn't have service. Or maybe he was coming up with another dumb scheme to win her back.

It didn't matter. It wasn't going to work.

She opened the door to her suite and made sure to lock it behind her. She felt exhausted, but she didn't want to sit down on the off chance that James was on his way.

Luckily, her room was empty, so she could slip out of the dress and get back into her comfortable clothes. As she threw things back into her bag, her phone rang.

She froze before peering over to see who it was. It was just Greg.

"Hey, what's up?"

"Hey. I've got good news," he said. "There's a flight leaving Midway in two hours. It'll bring you right into Lansing. Do you think that you can make it?"

"Definitely," she said as she zipped up her bag.

"Okay good. It looks like there are six open seats and only one other standby passenger is listed. I'd say you've got a pretty good shot to get onto the flight."

"Thank you so much Greg, I can't tell you how much of a life-saver you are. I swear that I'll pay you back for the standby ticket."

He laughed. "Don't be ridiculous. It was like $20. Consider it a gift."

"I really don't – "

"Or consider it a consolation prize."

She shook her head, even though he couldn't see her. "I will send you the money, okay?"

"Fine," he relented. "Have a good flight! Let me know if you don't make it, I'll find another one."

"Thanks Greg."

Juliet ended the call and set a reminder on her phone to send a check to Greg and Kerry. Then, she picked up her bag and headed back downstairs; Reggie was still waiting for her.

"Hey Reg – would you mind taking me to Midway Airport?"

"It'd be my pleasure," he said as he opened the door for her.

There wasn't any traffic and she managed to get to the airport in half an hour. She thanked Reggie before heading inside to ticketing.

Her standby ticket was waiting for her there, and she got through security quickly. It wasn't until after she got a coffee that she allowed herself a moment to think.

As she sat in front of the gate, she sipped on the coffee and closed her eyes. Somehow she'd managed to avoid seeing James all this time. Hopefully, Reggie wouldn't tattle on her and tell him where she was.

It didn't matter, though. Her flight was supposed to start boarding soon, and she could go back to her apartment and lock the door so that he could never speak to her again.

That was what she wanted, wasn't it? She wanted an excuse to never speak to him again. She finally had it. He messed up so royally this time that he couldn't expect her to forgive him again.

Yet...why did she feel sad? It was more than just losing the money to save the clinic – though that made her exceedingly sad.

Juliet rubbed her face in her hands, but quickly pulled away when she remembered that she was wearing makeup.

"Oh shoot," she said, examining the black mascara smeared on her fingers. She delicately tried to wipe off the smudges around her eyes.

How was she supposed to feel? This whole thing with James was a fantasy. Just like when she dated him before, it was silly to believe that two people who were so different could ever make it work. It was silly of her to even entertain the idea.

Juliet was angry at him, and not just because he sabotaged her entry. It was everything about him and everything that he did.

He acted like he was different. He tried to be cute by buying all of those Combos and ginger ales; he apologized and made her laugh and joked about crying in front of his fireplace.

And for what? Just so he could remind her that every time she risked opening her heart, it was a mistake? That someone could pretend to be good, and kind, and generous and still be a total selfish jerk who always thinks he's right and ruins the only thing you care about?

Juliet felt tears rushing to her eyes. How could she have been so foolish to trust him again?

She took a deep breath and bit her lip. She was not going to cry over James Balin.

Not again.

He simply wasn't worth her tears.

Chapter 24

"I've never actually been up here before," said Brad.

"Yeah," responded James. "Now you can see that it's nothing special."

They were on the 45th floor waiting outside of the boardroom meeting. When James initially called his dad about needing to present to the board, he was met with resistance.

"You fall off the face of the earth for weeks and expect to come back in, no questions asked?"

"I've been working on something big," said James. It wasn't worth getting into an argument. "Do you want to see it or not?"

"Make it good. This is your only chance."

The line cut out. James knew that his dad hung up on him. He knew his dad was angry. He didn't care – his only goal was to make sure that Juliet's clinic was funded. One way or another, he would achieve this goal.

They could hear laughter and voices from inside the boardroom, but they couldn't make out what was being said. James knew what his dad was doing – he was purposely keeping him waiting to teach him his place. James wouldn't let it rattle him.

After waiting for 40 minutes, the door finally opened.

Brad looked at him with wide eyes. "Are we up?"

James nodded. "Don't worry. I'll do most of the talking. Except for when some legitimate science comes up – you know, the stuff that actually matters."

Brad laughed nervously. "I can definitely speak to the science."

"That'll be perfect."

"Hello everyone," James said as they walked into the board room.

"Hey Jimmy, long time no see," responded Eric.

"Good to see you, Eric."

James ignored the nickname. Eric was trying to push his buttons – obviously, he took his lead from the boss. James didn't take it personally. He ignored their chatter as he connected his laptop to the projector. It only took him a few minutes to get his presentation loaded; Brad handed out packets that contained all of the slides and background numbers.

He cleared his throat. "Ladies and gentlemen of the board – and Dad."

The room rippled with laughter.

James continued. "I'm here to present an overview of a new opportunity that stands to bring in an additional $40 million to Balin Labs next year."

He clicked the button on the projector to go to the first slide that read, "Untapped Opportunity."

"I'm sure you're asking yourself how I'm going to do that. Is it developing a new drug? Exploring a new disease state? Or, do I plan to rob a bank?"

Everyone in the room, except for his dad, chuckled.

He clicked to the next slide. "None of the above. My proposal requires minimal investment up front for a projected $300 million in revenue over the next five years."

With another click, Juliet's Delicaid video started playing. It was the shorter version – only three minutes long – and it gave James the opportunity to study the faces of the board members as they watched.

When the video was complete, Beverly, the only female member of the board, spoke first. "James, did you forget what company you work for?"

Everyone laughed. Good. They were still engaged.

"I didn't. What you just watched was an entry into a competition that the makers of Delicaid pulled off brilliantly. Their drug, which is mechanistically similar to our Tremibade product, has been used to treat cancer in a variety of animal species for the last seven years."

James surveyed the room for a moment. The laughter was replaced with expressions ranging from skepticism to interest.

"This is the part where I need to step aside," said James. "I'd like to introduce Brad Michelson, one of our top scientists. He's been involved with the development of Tremibade since the beginning. He's here to discuss the potential of the drug, and hopefully he won't confuse you *too* much."

Brad nodded enthusiastically. "Hopefully I won't confuse you at all. Now, what you need to understand about the basic pharmacokinetics of both of these drugs..."

James watched as Brad gave a high-level summary of the mechanisms of both drugs. Earlier that week, James made Brad practice his part of the presentation.

"You have to dumb it down enough," James advised, "so that even I can understand it."

It turned out that Brad overestimated James. It took four tries to finally get the presentation down to a dumb enough level.

"Are you sure they won't be insulted by this?" asked Brad.

James shook his head. "Trust me. They barely understand how any of these drugs work. I would know."

Brad got to the part of the presentation where some of the numbers expanded on the screen. Everyone in the audience let out an audible, "Wow."

Well, except James' father. He was as stony faced as ever.

James didn't let it deter him. It was time for him to conclude the presentation. He knew from experience that keeping it under 15 minutes was their best bet.

"Thanks Brad. And finally, I've got some numbers that show the projections for the demand of the drug. You can also find these in your packets."

"How would you propose that we would even implement something of this size?" asked Beverly.

James smiled. "Thank you for that question, I was hoping someone would ask that. As I'm sure you're all aware, veterinarians are able to prescribe medications once they are approved in humans. My plan, which starts on page 18 of your packet, details how we would incentivize veterinarians to not only use our drug in their patients but also to report the data that they collect."

"What kind of data?" asked Eric.

"Once we get through some initial safety testing, we can expand the number of clinics and get survival times, adverse effects, everything."

The board members turned and quietly murmured to one another, flipping through the pages of the packets. The room became animated again, and James' spirits lifted.

His father did not touch his packet. "James, I need to see you in my office."

"Thanks everyone, I'll be back soon," James said graciously.

He followed his dad out of the board room and into an office three doors down.

When the door was closed, his dad turned to him. "What in the world do you think you're doing?"

"I'm finding new areas of revenue for the business. Isn't that something you wanted?"

His dad slammed the packet onto his desk. "Don't be cute with me. I know what this is about. You've been running around with that girl again and she's got your head all twisted."

James pulled away. "That girl?"

"The veterinarian. Why can't you just let her go?"

"Have you been spying on me?"

"It's not spying when the future leader of my company is getting into car accidents in *my* car because his girlfriend told him to."

James felt like he'd been slapped in the face. "Excuse me? Is that what you think this is about?"

"Of course it is," he spat back.

"You wanted me to be serious – "

"Yeah, I want you to get serious about this company. Not this nonsense."

"The board didn't seem to think it was nonsense," retorted James.

"The board didn't start this company."

James could see that there was a vein popping out of his dad's head. "Whatever you want to do, Dad. I'm just presenting some ideas."

"And if you think you can sneak in some project to save your girlfriend's failure of a clinic, you need to think again."

"Is that what this is about to you? Making sure that I'm never happy?"

"This is nonsense!" he yelled. "You're behaving like a lovesick teenager. Get back to what you're good at. Sales."

James crossed his arms. "I'm sorry to hear that you didn't like my new idea. Unfortunately, I won't be getting back to sales. Today is my last day at the company."

"Oh, so now you're going to throw a tantrum to get your way? Typical."

"I'm not throwing a tantrum," James said calmly. "I've been thinking about this for a long time. I'm never going to be good enough for you. I'm never going to be happy here. So I'm moving on with my life."

His dad scoffed. "Moving on? Well good luck with that, you're not getting a penny from me."

"That's fine," said James. "Tomorrow morning I'm selling all of my shares in Balin Labs."

"Don't be ridiculous."

"I'm just letting you know," James said softly.

His dad pointed a finger at him. "You're going to tank our stock prices. I can see the headlines now – 'Heir to Balin Labs' Fortune Dumps Stock.' Can you imagine?"

James shrugged. "I can just sell a quarter of them tomorrow, if you prefer, and the rest in the weeks to come. You're welcome to buy them."

"I'm welcome to buy them!" his dad said, throwing his hands up and turning to look out the window. "This is what I get for spoiling you. You've always been ungrateful. I'm not talking to you when you're acting like this."

"Goodbye Dad," James said before turning to leave.

As disappointed as he was by his dad's reaction, he wasn't surprised. He had to move quickly to enact Plan B. He picked up his phone and dialed.

"Hey, Marie? Looks like I'm going to need that favor."

Chapter 25

With only a few weeks until the end of the year and the end of the clinic, Juliet had a lot of work to do. She spent an entire weekend printing out the records of every patient in the clinic so that the owners could have them to take to another veterinarian.

Her hope was that she could get some sort of grant funding to reopen the clinic, but that would be months away. Until then, her old patients would have to find help elsewhere.

It broke Juliet's heart.

She hadn't known about the other potential grants until James emailed her about them. She knew that he would eventually contact her, but she was surprised when she read his email. He didn't say anything about trying to make it up to her. He didn't even hint at it. He apologized for messing things up and said that he knew that sorry was not enough.

He also said that he spoke to Gracie who told him about several other grants, and he attached information in the email. The last line of his email said something cryptic about him being sure that the clinic would be saved.

That annoyed her. How did *he* know? He seemed to think that money would just come out of thin air. Typical James.

Part of the transition in closing the clinic included Juliet moving back in with her parents. This was a special sort of failure – it really rubbed salt in the wound.

Her mom was thrilled, of course, to have her back, and her dad didn't miss a chance to crack jokes about her returning to the nest.

As much as Juliet felt like a failure, she knew it would be harder for her to get funding for the clinic if she was also looking for a new job at the same time.

She figured it'd be better if she moonlighted at another clinic for a few hours a week so she could focus most of her time on grant proposals. Unfortunately, making that decision meant facing the fact she was not going to be able to make rent and pay her student loans at the same time.

Her landlord was relieved to hear that she was moving out. "Finally," he said when she told him.

She wanted to respond in a pithy way, but she didn't have a leg to stand on. She still owed the man two month's rent. One month would be covered by her security deposit, but she needed to come up with the money for the other.

So instead of saying something sassy, she said, "Aw come on, you're going to miss me when I'm gone."

"No," he said flatly. "I will have paying tenants."

"At least I didn't break anything."

He smiled, wagging a finger at her. "Don't get any ideas."

One nice thing was that she had the rest of the month to slowly move back to her parents' house. She decided to make the most of her last Christmas in the apartment. She put up her three foot tall plastic tree and dressed it with a six foot tree's worth of decorations.

She put lights around her bedroom window and strung garland around the kitchen and bathroom. It made her feel better – like there would be hope in the future.

The weekend before Christmas, she took some time to move a few larger items to her parents' house. She thought she could do this unnoticed, but her mom was very excited for her arrival and had a bunch of evergreen branches stacked in the kitchen.

"I thought we could make some wreathes!" she said.

The fresh smell of the branches was inviting. "Are these pine branches? Where did you get all of these, Mom?"

She smiled. "No, cypress. And wouldn't you like to know!"

Juliet laughed. She decided that it was better not to ask too many questions and instead just join in and make a wreath. Her brother was visiting with his family for Christmas, so that would be nice. She didn't have much money to get gifts for her niece and nephew, but luckily the toys that they asked for weren't terribly expensive. She also got some tools to build an igloo and snowmen outside. That could keep them occupied for the entirety of Christmas day.

Juliet rolled up her sleeves and got to work in making a wreath. "Seriously Mom, where'd you get these? Why is there so much sap?"

"That's how you know they're good branches."

"Oh my goodness," said Juliet. Her fingers were sticking together. "Listen Mom, I want you to know that I'm going to be a really good roommate. Did you and Dad decide on what rent you're going to charge me?"

"Yes we did," her mom answered. "One dollar a month."

"No Mom, I'm serious. I don't want to be an old, loser daughter living in the house. Let me contribute."

Her mom pursed her lips. "Honey, you know that I would pay you to get you to live in this house again, so there's no way in the world that your father and I are going to take money from you. We just want you to get back on your feet."

"I was going to say that your friend could get you a job," her dad yelled from the living room. "But it looks like he's out of a job, too!"

Juliet scrunched her eyebrows. "What friend?"

He walked into the kitchen holding a newspaper. "Your friend. James. This article said that he left his dad's company."

"What?" Juliet reached to grab the paper, her fingers instantly bonding to the thin pages. "Since when do you read the investment stuff?"

He shrugged. "I'm a mysterious man."

Her mom scoffed. Juliet focused on reading the headline that read "Billionaire Heir Sells Stock and Says Sayonara to Family Business."

She quickly read the first two paragraphs, but when she tried to turn the page, she ripped the thin paper in her hand.

"Hey!" her dad said. "I'm not done with that! Don't go destroying it with your sticky fingers."

"I can't help it. These branches mom got are so sappy."

"Probably because she cut them at the park."

Juliet shot her mother a look. "Mom, you didn't!"

"You should never listen to your father," her mom said, continuing her work.

"What does it say, Dad? Did James get fired?"

"No, nothing like that. Doesn't really say why he left. It's making people nervous, though. It's not a good sign when your own son flees the company."

"So he really wasn't kidding about being fired..." Juliet mumbled to herself.

"What was that?" her mom asked.

"Nothing," she added quickly, handing the newspaper back to her dad.

It was no business of hers what James was up to. Good for him, if leaving was what he wanted. If not – well, at least he saw it coming.

Her dad turned to leave but her mom flagged him down. "Go up to Juliet's room and give her the mail that's been arriving here."

Juliet turned to her mom. "What kind of mail? How am I getting mail here already?"

"Because your mom started forwarding it from your old address," responded her dad. "And she was hoping you wouldn't notice."

Juliet turned back to her mom, who was expertly avoiding eye contact.

"Mom," she said, "is this true? I was wondering why I wasn't getting any mail at my apartment."

"It can take some time for mail to start forwarding. I'm just trying to be helpful, so sue me!"

Juliet went to the sink to wash her hands. "Don't worry Dad, I'll go look myself."

She managed to get a fair amount of the sap off before she went to her room. There was a stack of letters sitting on her bed. She groaned – she should have known something like this was going on when she didn't get a single Christmas card in the mail.

Juliet took a seat and started sorting through the mail. Most of it was junk, which made it easy. There was one letter about her student loans – they were sold again and the interest rate was raised, again.

There was a handwritten thank you from one of her clients at the clinic. She couldn't finish reading it because she wanted to cry, so she set it aside for later.

The last was a letter from a place called Animal Agency, Inc. Juliet frowned. She never heard of this place before. She ripped open the letter and read the first few lines:

Dear Dr. McCarron,

We would like to congratulate you for your clinic's nomination for our Underserved Care Award. We became aware of your phenomenal efforts to keep your veterinary clinic running through an anonymous nomination. Our panel made the decision to grant your clinic a $3 million grant to be dispersed over the next six years at your discretion.

Her jaw dropped. Was this some kind of joke? She rushed back downstairs.

"Mom! Where's your computer?"

"I don't want you putting any viruses on there," she said.

"I'm not going to put any viruses on it," Juliet responded, trying to control her tone. "Where is it?"

"It's by my bed. But I'm serious – don't download anything!"

Juliet ran to her parents' bedroom, grabbing the laptop from the nightstand. She Googled the name of the company and quickly found a website.

It seemed like it was a legitimate place! They had several grants that they awarded every year. It looked like the last winner of this grant was from five years ago. Did funding run out for a while?

It didn't matter – it seemed like this might be real. She ran back into the kitchen yelling her head off. "We got funding! We actually got funding!"

"That's great honey! See, I knew you could do it!" Her mom paused. "Does this mean you're not moving back home?"

Juliet cringed. "Actually – my landlord kicked me out. So...I still need somewhere to crash for a bit."

A smile spread across her mom's face. "I'm so happy for you!"

"Thank you," Juliet said breathlessly. "I can't believe this is real."

Where did this come from? Who nominated her? And more importantly...where did the money come from? Juliet felt uneasy about it all. She didn't want to bring up her concerns to her parents, though. Instead, she decided to get back to her apartment for some more investigation.

Chapter 26

"I'm sorry man, I was told you weren't allowed back inside."

James stood, arms outstretched. "C'mon Tony! You know me. I'm not going to cause a trouble. I just want to grab a few of my things."

Tony shook his head. "I just can't, man."

"What if you went on break for 15 minutes and I happened to slip by?"

"You know," Tony said with a smile, "I am due for a break. Overdue, actually."

"Well I'm going to head outside then," said James. "I don't want to get in the way of your work."

Tony laughed before turning to walk into the break room.

James waited until he was out of sight to call the elevator. Tony was the head doorman in his building for the last four years. They always got along well – sometimes James even brought home an extra take-out meal for Tony when he knew he was working long shifts.

That was one of the things that James' dad couldn't anticipate – he was able to freeze the bank accounts, take cars, and essentially kick him out of the condo. But James still had a few tricks up his sleeve.

He got onto the elevator and went straight up. Luckily, there were only a few more things to pack. His dad would never know – in a week, there would be a new senior manager of sales living in this condo.

James' dad seemed to think that he was punishing him by taking everything away. It was embarrassing – like what a parent would do to their misbehaving ten year old, taking away all of their toys.

He thought it would convince James to come back to the company, to come to his senses. But it was having the opposite effect. James had never felt more free in his life. His duties to the company were over and he made as quiet of an exit as could be expected.

As agreed, he'd only sold off a quarter of his stock. The rest would come later – or never. He didn't care. He didn't want the money.

He had enough money for what he planned to do next. He put a deposit down on an apartment in Michigan. It wasn't that he was trying to be close to Juliet – that was sadly something he had to give up on. She never answered his email, and she apparently didn't figure out that he was the one who funded the charity that ultimately gave her clinic a grant.

It was better that way. If she had any idea where the money came from, she would probably refuse it. At least this way the clinic was saved. That was all that mattered. She'd given him a second chance, and he messed it up. That was his own fault. But he still wanted her to be happy.

No – he was moving back to Michigan to go back to school. He was sick of being miserable with his life. He was going back to school to get a degree in zoology. A surprising number of his credits still counted towards the degree, so he only had about two years of coursework left. He never even looked into it until now. How had he allowed his life to be on hold for so long?

He spent the next hour packing up his last few belongings. He just needed to load them into the moving truck and he would be on his way.

There was a knock at the door. James froze. Was Tony coming to kick him out? If that were the case, then he could at least help him carry some of the boxes down.

James swung the door open. "Alright, alright, I'm done packing my – "

James froze. It was Tony – but he wasn't alone.

"Hey, this young lady was downstairs looking for you," said Tony. "Do you know her?"

James couldn't believe what he was seeing. Was he actually hallucinating? Was his dad right and he'd actually lost his mind?

"Yes. I do. She's a friend."

Tony sighed. "Okay man, but I really need you out of here."

"Right, everything's packed up, I just need a few minutes?"

"One hour!" Tony said, pointing at him. "Don't make me call the police. You know I will!"

James laughed. "Got it. One hour."

Tony walked back to the elevator, leaving James to gape at Juliet. She smiled. "Hey."

He reminded himself to shut his mouth. "Hey! It's so nice to see you. Please come in."

She looked back at Tony, who was now getting on the elevator. "Are you sure it's okay? Is he really going to call the police?"

James waved a hand. "Nah. We just like to – you know, joke around about that."

Juliet peered into the condo. "It looks like all of your stuff is gone."

"Yeah, I'm moving out." He cleared his throat. "Please, come in."

She stepped inside and James closed the door behind her.

"Sorry it's so desolate in here," he said. "I think I have some soda in the fridge?"

She put up a hand. "No, I'm fine. Thank you though."

"I'm surprised that you remembered where I lived."

"Oh, I didn't," she said. "I looked it up online. It wasn't hard to find."

"Oh, duh."

They stood and looked at each other for a moment.

James couldn't stand the silence. "So what brings you to New York? I think you are literally the last person on earth I expected to come knocking at my door. To be honest, it was much more likely to be the NYPD."

She laughed. "Yeah, sorry."

He scratched the back of his head. "No, I didn't mean – I'm happy to see you."

"So where are you moving?"

"Back to school."

"Oh?"

"In Michigan," he added quickly, "but just because I found out that I only need four more semesters to finish a zoology degree."

"Oh!" Juliet said. "That's a big change."

He nodded. "It is. It's a long time coming."

Juliet took a few more steps into the apartment, getting close enough to look out of one of the windows. "I thought you were kidding when you kept saying that you were going to get fired."

"I wasn't kidding," he said. "It was more of a wish, really."

Juliet bit her lip. "I see that. So your dad really fired you?"

James crossed his arms. "It's hard to say what happened. Some words were exchanged. I guess, technically, I quit."

"So you can't collect unemployment now," she said with a smirk.

"Exactly. I kept trying to get fired and couldn't. But I think he may never speak to me again, so that's something."

"Oh," she said with a frown.

"Don't feel bad. It's better this way." He pulled a large box over to Juliet. "Have a seat. Best box in the house."

"No, thank you. I don't want to take up too much of your time. I just wanted to thank you."

He raised an eyebrow. "Thank me?"

"Don't pretend like you don't know. I found out about you selling your stock in the company. The same day that I found out my clinic was anonymously nominated for a grant."

James opened his mouth, trying to appear shocked. "What! That's amazing, so you can keep the clinic open?"

She crossed her arms. "Don't play dumb with me!"

"I would never! And I know that you would never accept money from me, so I don't know why you think that I'm involved."

"Wait, are you serious?" she said, her cheeks turning slightly pink.

Well that made him feel bad. He couldn't lie to her. "No, I'm not serious. I was just hoping you wouldn't figure it out."

She lightly poked him in the shoulder. "You almost had me."

"Please don't tell me you came all this way to try to return the money. Because that is legitimate charity, and if you refuse it, they'll just have to give it to another clinic."

"I know," she said. "I investigated them quite thoroughly. I actually came to the city to meet with someone from their office. It seems that your donation funded fifteen other clinics across the country."

"You investigated? You don't joke around, do you?" said James.

She shook her head. "Not when it comes to my clinic. Now, they did try to hide who the donation was from, but it wasn't hard to figure out. So basically, what I guess I'm trying to say is – thank you."

James smiled. "You're welcome. I'm glad that I was able to not mess something up. There's a first time for everything."

"Ha. Right. Well, I wanted to apologize, too. I realize that you were just trying to help with the Delicaid competition."

James rubbed his forehead. "Yeah, I mean I was, but I did it in a stupid way. I should've kept my nose out of it. You were going to win on your own."

Juliet shook her head. "I mean, I don't know about that."

"Kylie made it *pretty* obvious," said James. "I underestimated the grudge she held against me."

"What'd you do to her?" Juliet cocked her head to the side.

"Well, uh – she kind of had a thing for me."

A smile spread across Juliet's face. "Ah, right. I can see that. A woman scorned and all."

He nodded. "Yeah, and I thought she was nice. For an employee, nothing more. She kept bringing in these danishes, I guess she read in a magazine that I really liked danishes. It got weird."

Juliet stepped closer to him and brushed against his hand. James felt his heart jump.

"You didn't like Kylie, then?" she asked.

He didn't want to keep harping on how he'd only loved her for all of these years. But she *was* asking. "No, I had my heart set on someone else."

"Oh," she said, stepping away. "I see."

He took a chance and grabbed her hand. "It was you, Juliet. I don't want to keep pestering you with my feelings – I promise I won't bring it up again. But I just...wanted you to know. It's always been you."

She squeezed his hand. "I know."

He felt like a window was opening. He didn't know why or how, and he hadn't expected it, but he wasn't going to let it slip away. He took her other hand in his.

"And if you were to tell me that you even felt a fraction of that for me, even if it just came on in the last day or so..."

A smile spread across her face. "And what if I did tell you that?"

"Then I'd have to kiss you."

She leaned in. "Well, we wouldn't want that, would we?"

"No," he said, gently touching her face. "We wouldn't."

He couldn't resist it any more – he closed his eyes and kissed her. To his surprise, she kissed him back. His heart soared – it was worth the wait.

"You had to keep me guessing until the last second, didn't you?" he asked, unable to contain the smile on his face.

She shrugged. "I'm a mysterious woman."

"Can I be a mysterious man?"

"No," she said with a laugh. "Everything about you is pretty much all out there. Now would you kiss me again?"

She didn't have to ask twice – he wrapped his arms around her and pulled her in for another kiss.

Epilogue

That morning, Juliet got up early. She'd taken the day off of work, so she wanted to sleep in, but she was too excited. It was the one year anniversary of James starting his job as a zookeeper, and she was going to the zoo to see some sort of surprise that he set up.

She had no idea what it was going to be, but he promised that it had something to do with his favorite charges – the elephants – so she knew that whatever it was would be adorable. Juliet checked her phone to see if there were any updates from him. There was a text message. "Good morning sunshine! I left something for you on the doorstep – hopefully you get to it before the raccoons do."

She laughed. Her new apartment was nicer than her old one (and the landlord never yelled at her), but there were some very crafty raccoons that kept getting into her trash cans. She hopped out of bed and opened the front door. A box from her favorite bakery sat on the welcome mat. She carried it inside and opened the lid in the kitchen; it was full of croissants and pastries.

"That was risky," she typed on her phone. "The raccoons definitely would've enjoyed this. But thank you, because I'm going to enjoy it more!"

A cold nose pressed into the back of her calf. Juliet turned around to see that her dog Rufus was also interested in having some fresh pastries for breakfast.

She bent down and kissed his head. "This is not for you buddy."

He sat down, then tried to give paw. When that didn't work, he laid down and rolled over. Juliet laughed. She knew she couldn't allow herself to be manipulated by his cuteness, but it was tough.

"Alright, I won't give it to you now, but if you're really good and go sit in your bed and stop bothering me, I'll save you a little bite later."

He realized that she wasn't going to give in; though he didn't know what she said, he was still satisfied with this arrangement and took himself to go sit on the couch.

Juliet turned back to the bakery box. What was she supposed to do with all of these pastries? How many pastries could one woman eat?

This was very much an "old" James kind of move. He used to do things like this all the time when they were both in college. When James went back to finish his degree, it was like he was reborn. He started being thoughtful again, it was like he was filled with joy.

James finished all of his coursework in just 18 months. He was completely dedicated, and he spent much of his free time volunteering at the zoo in hopes of landing a full-time position when one opened up.

The rest of his time was spent with Juliet. The change in him was amazing and she couldn't help falling deeper in love with him. Her mind told her it was dangerous, but her heart couldn't resist.

At first she was concerned that he might want to return to his old life in New York City. His dad certainly put up a fight. First, he took away James' access to all of the comforts he'd grown used to – his condo, his cars, and the ridiculous piles of money.

James was unfazed. He was completely caught up in his schoolwork and loved all the classes he was taking. On top of that, he still had a *lot* of money from selling some of his shares in the company. It was more than enough to keep him comfortable – though his dad didn't think it would last because of James' history of poor spending habits. Luckily, Juliet was more than happy to teach him what a budget looked like.

The next step, then, was bribery. His dad told him that he could get a raise and more control of the company if he were to come back. James politely declined, telling him that he was very happy where he was.

That didn't go over well, and his father demanded to buy back all of the stocks that James controlled. James was happy to sell them off – but then his dad changed his mind.

After that failed to turn James back to the family business, his father resorted to pleading. He tried to use guilt, intermixed with occasional anger. Juliet thought that he was going through all the stages of grief.

"Unfortunately, he'll never get to acceptance," said James.

"I wouldn't be so sure about that," Juliet said.

When James graduated with his zoology degree, Juliet invited his dad to the graduation ceremony. She wasn't sure that he would come, but she thought it was worth a shot. He did end up coming, but he had the attitude that he was allowing James to have a bit of fantasy until he came back to his "real" life.

It wasn't until Juliet sent about fifty pictures and videos of James loving his new job at the zoo that his dad started to come around. It was enough time for him to see that the business was able to function without James. And it was enough time for him to see that James was serious and most importantly, that James was happy.

Juliet was glad that they were back on speaking terms. She knew that it might take years for them to mend their relationship, but at least they were on the right path.

And Juliet and James' relationship had never been better. On their one year anniversary, James convinced Juliet that it would be fun to go to the local animal shelter to look at the pets.

Juliet knew what he was doing – he was trying to trick her into getting another dog. She told him that she wasn't ready, and he said there was no pressure to adopt anyone, but that he just wanted to go look.

That's when she met Rufus. He was three years old and ended up in the shelter because his owner passed away. Juliet fell in love with him at once – he had the pointy ears of a German Shepherd, but he must've had some husky in him too because he had one blue and one brown eye. He barked at her incessantly until she came over to his cage to say hello. Then he sat there with a very pleased look on his face, trying to display his array of tricks.

She brought him home that day.

After eating two croissants, Juliet packed up some of the pastries and left to meet James at the zoo. She loved visiting him at work – everyone there loved him, and everyone there knew her. James mostly worked with the elephants now, but he also ran some educational classes for the children who came to the zoo on field trips. Juliet had never seen him happier in his entire life, and it was infectious.

She got to the elephant exhibit and looked around. James was nowhere to be seen, but two of the elephants were playing with toys in the enclosure. They both came running over when they saw Juliet.

"Hey ladies!" she said. "Have you seen James?"

Rosie, the older female, tried to give Juliet a bushel of branches.

Juliet laughed, stretching over the wall to accept them. A moat of water separated them, making it impossible to reach. "Rosie, I can't reach from here, but thank you."

She stood there talking to them for about 15 minutes until James emerged from the elephant house.

"Hey beautiful!" he yelled. "How long have you been waiting there?"

She shrugged. "Not long. And Rosie tried to feed me some branches, so I'm taken care of."

He laughed. "She's always loved you."

"Thank you for the baked goods, I brought you some leftovers."

"Oh, perfect! They were all for you, though."

"Me and the raccoons."

"Exactly." He walked to the edge of the enclosure. "Do you want to meet me at the door of the elephant house and I can show you what Rosie and I have been working on?"

"Sure."

Juliet walked over. James and Rosie greeted her once she reached the elephant house. She patted Rosie on the trunk and Rosie tried to play with her ponytail.

"So what's this big surprise?" asked Juliet.

"Well," said James, a broad smile spreading on his face, "I was talking to some other keepers about how they enrich the lives of their elephants. They said that some of them really like painting on canvas."

"I've seen this online!" said Juliet. "It's really funny."

"Yeah! She's been painting away for the last three weeks, but today she doesn't feel like it. I was hoping you could walk in and see her with a paintbrush in her trunk."

Juliet laughed. "She's entitled to do what she wants with her time."

"I know, and right now all she cares about is trying to undo your ponytail. But I can show you some of the paintings that she made earlier?"

He led her into a back room that had canvases stacked up on a table. "This is the first one that she did – I think she was trying to paint some tall grasses here. They're not green, obviously she only had orange paint, but clearly these are orange grasses."

"Yeah, I see it."

He moved it to the side to show the next canvas. "Now this one I can kind of see as a self-portrait. I think she was really trying to paint just her ear, though."

Juliet laughed – he was being so funny about this. "Yes, definitely."

He shifted the canvas to the side. The next one was a yellow circle. Juliet picked it up. "Wow, did she do this one?"

James shook his head. "No, that was me showing her what the paintbrushes could do."

"Oh I see." Juliet set it aside and reached for the next canvas. Her heart skipped a beat. This one had another yellow circle, plus some words written on the top: Juliet, will you marry me?

She looked over at James to see that he was down on one knee, an open ring box in his hand.

"That one was me too," he said. "But Rosie really encouraged me to do it. She said that you make me a better man, and that everything in my life has improved because of you. She said that you're the best thing that ever happened to me. And I think she's right. I love you endlessly. Will you do me the honor of being my wife?"

Juliet dropped to her knees to be on eye level with him. "I think Rosie is right. And yes!"

He swept her into his arms and carried her into the elephant enclosure. "Good news Rosie! She said yes!"

Rosie seemed interested as to why Juliet was being carried around. She started playing with Juliet's ponytail again and Juliet felt like she was being patted on the head. She burst into laughter.

"I must say, you did much better this time with the proposal."

He pulled away with a smirk on his face. "I've always been a slow learner."

"Better late than never," she said, leaning in for a kiss.

Author's Note

Thanks for reading! I'd love to know what you thought, and reader reviews are one of the most influential factors in whether someone will give a book a chance. So, if you've enjoyed this book, would you please consider reviewing it?

Would you like to read my free novella?

Sign up for my newsletter and get a copy of my free novella "Falling for my Brother's Billionaire Best Friend." I use my newsletter to send updates about new releases and sales! Oh, and to tell embarrassing stories about my husband. You can sign up by visiting: http://bit.ly/billionairestory

About the Author

Amelia Addler writes always clean, always swoon-worthy romance stories and believes that everyone deserves their own happily ever after.

Her soulmate is a man who once spent five weeks driving her to work at 4AM after her car broke down (and he didn't complain, not even once). She is lucky enough to be married to that man and they live in Pittsburgh with their little yellow mutt. Visit her website at AmeliaAddler.com or drop her an email at AmeliaAddler@gmail.com.

Also by Amelia...

The Westcott Bay Series

Saltwater Cove

Saltwater Studios

Saltwater Secrets

Saltwater Crossing

Saltwater Falls

Christmas at Saltwater Cove

The Billionaire Date Book Series

Nurse's Date with a Billionaire

Doctor's Date with a Billionaire

Veterinarian's Date with a Billionaire

Made in the USA
Las Vegas, NV
17 August 2023

76218965R10122